KEY TO THE HIGHWAY

RICHARD ANDREWS

Untimely Books

Untimely Books

untimelybooks.com
An imprint of Cosmos Cooperative
PO Box 3, Longmont, Colorado 80502
info@untimelybooks.com

Book design by Kayla Morelli
Cover art by Vytas Kapociunas vytasfineart.com
Vesica art by Anthony Morelli @greensoapandham

This is a work of fiction. Names, characters, places, and incidents either are the product of the author's imagination or are used fictitiously, and any resemblance to actual persons, living or dead, businesses, companies, events, or locales is entirely coincidental.

Publisher Cataloging-in-Publication Data
Names: Andrews, Richard, 1947 March 18-, author.
Title: Key to the Highway / Richard Andrews.
Description: Longmont, CO : Untimely Books, 2023. | Summary:
    An erotic motorbike fantasy and a magical blues harp take Chris
    Hunter on a wild, Orphic odyssey through the Australian Outback
    to Indonesia, India, Bangkok, Borneo and Rio. His reality morphs
    into a mythological world of gods and demons, manifested as bikers,
    prophets, gun runners, drug smugglers, shady businessmen and
    neo-Nazis. Empowered by an ancient esoteric secret, his journey to
    self-discovery climaxes in a battle with Alt-Right forces.
Identifiers: LCCN 2023939208 | ISBN 9781961334991 (paperback)
    9781961334007 (hardback) 9781961334984 (ebook)
Subjects: LCSH: Quests (Expeditions) -- Fiction. | Self-realization
    -- Fiction. | Good and evil -- Fiction. | LCGFT: Road fiction.
    | Mythological fiction. | BISAC: FICTION / Visionary &
    Metaphysical.
Classification: DDC 813.6
LC record available at https://lccn.loc.gov/2023939208

PRAISE FOR
KEY TO THE HIGHWAY

"*Key to the Highway* has moments of intensity and insight and a feel for the world and those years we all went out looking for something big in the far corners and hidden nooks, and lived with abandon, living like every song was the most important one. Parts of it took me right back to those days."

Carl Hoffman, author of *Savage Harvest, The Last Wild Men of Borneo*, and *Liar's Circus*

"A fast-paced episodic adventure tale, with the narrator's harmonica providing an endless variety of entertaining ways to get him into and out of trouble."

Brendan Power, composer, recording artist, harpmeister for Sting and Van Morrison

"Evocative and astute observations about home, travelling and a life lived to the full. The driving rhythm of the music, which creates a great ambient sound throughout the novel, is a wonderful structural device as well as being such an encompassing central theme."

Jonathan Holmes, School of Creative Arts and Media, University of Tasmania

"This is an extraordinary romp of the Hero's Journey, so strap yourselves in!"

Dr. Grant Caldwell, School of Culture and
Communication, University of Melbourne

"A page-turning journey around the globe that reminds us to follow our heart and seize the day. Andrews beautifully captures the magic of being on an adventure; chance encounters, close calls and the traveler's notion of connection with the universe. The writing is invigorating, making this captivating story a great page turner. Although I'm a younger reader, I still enjoyed the '70s blues and biker universe mixed with the Greek classics and other ancient gods. Turning the last page left me sad that the blues odyssey had ended and at the same time inspired me to follow my passion."

Thor F. Jensen, Danish adventurer, writer
and award-winning explorer

"Richard Andrews' *Key to the Highway* is fresh and original. He spins an enthralling tale that merges the haunting strains of the blues with the kind of wild journeys that many of us dreamed of in the 1970s and '80s. We travel with him from the vast spaces of Outback Australia through the colour and chaos of Asia to end in South America. It's a fascinating journey accompanied by the roar of motorbikes and the music of the mysterious harmonica."

Margaret Farrell, journalist and travel photographer

"Read it in one go. Loved it! Key to the Highway is a voyage of self-discovery as seen through actual events. This is the book for you if romping through the freedom of one's childhood in post-war Australia, a taste of the hippie trail and winging it on gut feeling is to your liking."

Clive Scott, traveller, raconteur

"Couldn't stop reading it! Really well written. [*Key to the Highway* kept] the action going and the pacing is great."

Angela Leuck, Tanka poet and author
of *More Grows in a Crooked Row*

"An edgy novel with quirky, realistic characters, confrontations, caustic observations, and vivid scenes, *Key to the Highway* unlocks inner desires, and exposes the nature of friendships, love and ambition."

Kevin McQuillan, Melbourne writer and television producer

"The reader is bombarded with allusions to ancient Greek and Roman myths, to Yemanja worshipped by African slaves transported to Brazil, to Sanskrit poems and to threads of the Aboriginal Dreamtime. Freya and Lockie, gods from the Norse Tree of Life are also referenced. These allusions serve to underline Chris' quest and to remind us of its karmic nature. In each of his significant settings the author provides a quirky vignette to intensify the context, which imbues the account with drama and humour."

Bruce Tamagno, writer and geographer

To Marie, my Muse and Fellow Traveller:
Thy aid was the Key to my 'advent'rous Song'

"Death closes all: but something ere the end,
Some work of noble note, may yet be done,
Not unbecoming men that strove with Gods."

—Alfred, Lord Tennyson, *Ulysses*

"Travel far enough, you meet yourself."

—David Mitchell

"Harmonica helps me escape reality."

—*Slogan on T-shirt sold by Amazon*

CONTENTS

FOREWORD

My friend Tom was an ex-biker who quoted the classics, played blues and sometimes sold his paintings. We returned from long journeys one winter and shared a shabby bedsit in London.

One cold, wet evening, Tom stopped eating his Spam dinner, surrendered our last coin to the power meter and asked:

"What would it take, to return home just once, fit and tanned on a new BMW, with a gorgeous companion on the back—instead of turning up broke and scrawny on the Hackney bus?"

I lost contact with Tom when we travelled on. But his question was the genesis of a fantasy that took over my life.

Mate, if you're reading this book, here's how it goes...

IN THE BEGINNING...

Midnight. Pacific Highway. By the ocean that links the dreamtimes of ancient continents. A sensual, summer night when anything is possible. Youth before the Fall.

The sea breeze carries a distant drumbeat. A call for freedom shipped to Brazil with the Yoruban slaves. The rhythm builds up, joined by the song of the Amazon rainforest. The voices of the primeval jungle greet the slaves who escaped the plantations.

The music flows from a speeding white motorbike, bathed in lights. A searing blues harmonica soars like a condor above the Arion Custom and swoops over the mountain. The 1100 cc engine throbs a bass counterpoint. It changes key as the bike descends from the heavens.

The rider appears alone. A centaur on wheels. But as he leans into the bend, a figure with long, dark hair emerges. She holds him closely. A tress of hair blows forward to caress his face. The scent lingers a moment and then wafts away.

Aroused, the bike hugs the curves of the road as the bay opens up. The full moon sambas on a million ripples. Like Rio's floating candles that drift out to the sea goddess, Yemanja. Worshippers swirl and chant along the distant ocean of Atlantis. Her spirit enters their bodies.

The road straightens out and the woman presses closer. As the tacho nudges red, the beast's high octane energy flows through the rider. The drums crescendo as the wind carries him beyond the horizon. He has joined the gods. Invincible!

The alarm buzzes. Back to earth.

SHOWTIME

Cheap wine, dope and clove cigarettes now perfume what was once the roughest pub in Melbourne's inner suburbs. A stripped-back wooden floor has replaced the white tiles in the public bar, which previously allowed the day's piss and blood to be hosed away after closing.

The Camelot Hotel's new décor looks like a Templars' shopping spree in Furniture City. Refectory tables and high-backed wooden chairs line up against walls that sport shields and crossed swords. A wrought-iron chandelier with electric candles hangs from a ceiling beam by three black chains—thick enough to support the owner on the late nights he forgets his mission to change the hotel's raffish image.

A tough, Cretan lawyer has converted the labyrinth of rooms and passageways into a sanctuary for his three main passions: music, drinking and tax minimisation.

I'm fronting HellHound, the house band. We play a mixed bag of Chicago blues, Afro-Latin and Rock-Goes-East. The place is packed out tonight and the crowd's intoxicated energy fires up the group. A Malaysian didgeridoo player had joined us for the last set, droning an eerie mix of music that flowed from the Murray River to the Mississippi. Rami was an exchange student who skipped TESOL classes to go feral and learn circular breathing.

We finish a Muddy Waters bracket and Dion gives me the nod from behind the bar. It's time for *his* song. I nod back, but don't look forward to it. Just after hiring the group, he challenged us to play a tango, of all things. Ignoring my scepticism, he'd thrust the yellowing notes of an old Astor Piazzolla number into my hands.

"Try it!"

You learn to say yes, to keep a regular gig.

It took a solid week to adapt the bandoneon parts for harmonica and master the complex runs. Good for technique, but will it go down well with a hipster audience? Laszlo the guitarist is the only band member not worried about appearing uncool.

"It'll take me back to my roots," he jokes. "I learned that song years ago on violin. Tango works if you forget shopping-mall muzak and think Buenos Aires desperates."

The crowd is buzzing with anticipation for the next set. I squeeze past the bass player's wheelchair and step up to the mike.

"We're going to play another blues." (Cheers.)

"Not from Chicago this time, but the bars and brothels of Argentina." (More cheers.)

"It's called Libertango."

Smirks and disbelieving groans.

Laszlo ignores the response. He unstraps his guitar, shoulders an electric violin and winds up the amp.

"If old Astor got death threats for playing this number, we'll have to do it justice."

I take a deep breath and start a long, slow, minor run. The come-on. A taunting violin responds. The notes circle and tease each other with hints of the pleasures in store. Harp and violin move closer together and the two competing melodies become one. Bass and drums join the thrusting tempo.

The dark melody carries us to the poor, violent carnality of the Rio de la Plata waterfront. A song fed by the longing and suffering of 19th-century immigrant workers. Ghosts of knife-wielding compraditos strut the smoky room. In a deadly dance they contend for the favours of a beautiful woman. Harp duels violin as Laszlo and I trade solos against the heartbeat of the bass. The drums acclaim each clash and peak.

I'm wielding my Excalibur: a solid metal chromatic that unleashes four octaves plus that bend like a dream. The wailing notes take on a life of their own, sounding possessed, bereaved, wild. They cut through the air and ricochet off the walls. We play to exhaustion and climax on a discord that crashes like an overturned bar table. Stunned silence in the audience. Then loud applause.

Dion smiles, satisfied. But I have an uncomfortable feeling we've invoked a dark spirit that could turn nasty. Still, I grin at Laszlo in relief.

"That was great," he says, flicking a sweaty brown lock from his eyes. "You really had me going."

"I'm not sure what happened there, señor, but it's certainly thirsty work."

I announce a break. With a dry mouth I look towards the bar. She's sitting alone at a small table. A classic beauty with piercing dark eyes, long black hair and a lithe figure under a black leather jacket. She catches my eye with a glance that hints we already know each other. I mime the suggestion we share a drink. She agrees.

As I push my way through the crowd, a brown-shirted man leans over the table and whispers in her ear. His shaved head, pointed beard and solid, bullish shoulders look threatening. She shakes her head. He holds her shoulder and becomes more insistent. She turns away to ignore him. By the time I reach them he's bellowing.

"Then, why don't you go back to where you came from, you fucking Asian immigrant bitch!"

Dion had warned me that while I was away the national mood had mildewed into a breeding ground for semi-humans.

She sips her glass and pretends not to hear, hoping he'll just stomp away. The fascist rant continues. I stride up to him, still holding the harp. My hand is clenched white.

"Okay, pal, that's enough. You got your sacrifice."

Bull-man straightens, squares himself and eyes me up and down. Bad news. He's twice my size. A shield-shaped badge on his barrel chest proclaims **Single Society** in black Gothic lettering.

"Piss off, *pal*," he sneers. "Stick to blowing wog music on your mouth-organ."

My temper peaks in the red. I stand my ground. The crowd steps back.

"All right, you've made your point."

Bull-man snorts. "Here's another fucking point!"

He grabs a bottle from the nearby bar and smashes the end.

"What, no foreplay?"

Bull-man crouches forward. He jabs the jagged gape towards me. I have one chance. I swing the harp backhanded as hard as I can into his nose. The metal mouthpiece rasps across the bridge bone. A loud crunch accompanies a C major chord as his nostrils exhale through the blood and mucus. (Or was that a C augmented?)

"Not bad for a beginner. But you need practice."

Alerted by the noise, Janus the door-keeper pushes through the onlookers and drags the fallen monster outside. Dion picks up the phone and calls an ambulance. He makes a second call. Liquor bills for the Licensing Squad have just been discounted.

The bakelite receiver is slammed down and scores another crack.

"Chris, your hair-trigger and smart-assed comments will get you into real trouble one day. And I won't be able to help you."

"Thanks, Dion. Can I just have a drink?"

I hold up the harp and inspect the ooze dripping from holes one to ten.

"Actually, I'll need two tall glasses. One Jack Daniel's and one of the house rot-gut."

Dion puts his palms together in mock prayer.

"Save me. You've done Theseus and the Minotaur, a B-grade western, and now it's the Robert Johnson fantasy. Bluesman-defeats-Devil-drinks-big-whisky."

"Mate, give me a break. Can we cut the commentary from the Greek chorus, just for tonight? I'm not up to it."

He pushes the drinks across the bar. I swirl the harp in the Jack Daniel's. It turns murky. I down the other glass in one shot. Sita watches Mr. Smooth in action.

"Thank you," she says, when I finally sit down at her table. "Those people have been giving us a hard time lately. Ever since their candidate got elected."

We introduce ourselves. After what's happened, we laugh at the formal requirements of the belated exchange.

"I haven't seen you here before," I say, wincing a bit. It's not my best line.

"I've been travelling. I heard about this place only a few days ago. The music's terrific."

"Thanks. I hope I don't have to play the last little number again."

We cast around for a more pleasant topic. I withdraw my harp from the glass and wipe it dry with a paper napkin. She points to the symbol engraved on the cover plate. And tattooed on the back of my hand.

"What's the significance of that? Reminds me of an Indian mandala."

"It's a long story."

She leans towards me.

"We have world enough and time."

Thanks for the line, Mr. Marvell. No coyness there.

CALL TO ADVENTURE

I suppose the journey really started in bayside Melbourne, where I grew up by the Kananook Creek. Not very wide or deep, but the swampy waterway served as the Amazon, Nile and Ganges to a young boy seeking adventure in the button-down 1950s. The Kananook flowed past suburban backyards on one side and a nature reserve on the other. Across the creek from my place, a ravine opened onto a flat, sandy bank. Just up the road stood the Avalon Milk Bar and a public phone box. A rickety, wooden footbridge crossed the water behind them.

A small order of knights had claimed the kingdom. Thorry, Laszlo, Gary and I built a hut in the bush for secret meetings. A discarded cable drum served as round table and we fortified the place with other regalia found at the tip. We trained as true warriors and modelled ourselves on different heroes. Gary stuck to Sir Gawain as his favourite alter ego. The surrounding trees were scarred from knives, spears, sharpened screwdrivers; whatever weapons came to hand.

Sword fights were based on gladiator sagas in Vistavision, while a TV replay of an old Tarzan movie inspired blow-guns made from plastic tubing. Curare was in short supply, so we smeared the poison darts with Vegemite.

The latest fad was *shanghais*, or slingshots, using tree forks, tyre-tubes and the leather tongues of old shoes. The thickness of the rubber bands was a status symbol. It measured the strength a knight needed to pull back the leather pouch. Local wildlife and street-lights were fortunate that the most powerful slingshots were difficult to steady and aim. I chose a lighter version, that turned out to be deadly accurate.

Once, I brought down a black water-hen flying overhead and watched her die an agonising death, screaming and thrashing around in the water. Just a quick shot, without really aiming, which broke her neck. Still twitching, the black form floated away with the current to create my first awareness of cruelty and death.

I stopped firing at birds, but learned you pay for such wanton acts.

That January was oppressively hot and the summer holidays were starting to drag on. I spent days alone at home reading illustrated versions of ancient epics in the pile of Classic Comics I'd swapped for my Phantom collection.

Thorry and Laszlo dropped by with a treasure-trove of large lightbulbs taken from a construction site. We floated them down the creek for target practice, exulting in the explosions from a direct hit.

After smashing all the lightbulbs, we needed something else to do. Or destroy. Another group of boys our age arrived on the opposite bank. They started kicking an old yellow football around.

"Hey, that's our golden ball," said an outraged Laszlo.

"Those *infidels* must have found our hut and raided it!" I said, using a word I'd just learned.

"Let's get it back," thundered Thorry, ever ready for a battle.

In all good wars the cause gets lost in the ensuing events, which develop their own momentum. We started with insults and accusations hurled across the creek with escalating intensity. After exhausting the repertoire, one of the looters recognised Thorry and decided to play dirty.

"Yeah, well, my big brother screwed your sister in the back of his Holden at the drive-in during the Val Morgan ad for Tim Tams. She couldn't even wait for the film to start. He reckons she's a harlot. *H*elen the *H*arlot!"

The circumstantial details, capped off with the exaggerated *H* alliteration, launched Thorry's fury. He unsheathed his shanghai and fired a sharp rock at the tormentor. Hand cupped around the ear, waiting for the scream.

And then it was on!

The enemy was armed and returned fire. Stones whizzed around us. We had the advantage of thick cover on our side, while they had to expose themselves on the open bank if they wanted to close in for a decent shot.

When it got too dark to see, Thorry yelled out: "Come back tomorrow, if you're not too chicken."

"We'll be here. Why don't you bring your sister? She's more accurate with her fork than you are!"

We were having a great time.

The three of us returned to the battlefront the next morning to find a fort on the further bank thrown together from rusty sheets of corrugated iron and bits of wood. Not only had they raided our hut, they'd dismantled it as well. An insult that equalled any jibe about Thorry's sister and her questionable appreciation of cinema.

The battle resumed with increased ferocity. Nearby council roadworks provided a large munitions supply and we pillaged neighbourhood dustbin lids, for shields.

By high noon, the battle reached a stalemate.

We couldn't dislodge the enemy; the taunts were getting repetitious and no one had been properly injured. Laszlo had assured his parents he was playing basketball, but they were making ominous noises about neglected violin practice. Unless we acted soon, history would record no heroic deeds.

I remembered a battle in one of the Classic Comics and convened a knight's assembly.

"Let's call Gary, sneak him into one of our positions, so it looks like there's still only three on our side. Then one of us can attack from behind."

Thorry and Laszlo were enthusiastic.

"It's a dangerous mission," said Thorry in his best Ancient Leader voice.

"But you're the best shot, Chris. And it was your idea," added Laszlo.

I ran to the phone box and called Gary. Pedalling furiously, he arrived on his Malvern Star within minutes, glad for the diversion from cleaning out his dad's back shed.

While Thorry and Laszlo kept firing, Gary helped prepare me for the mission.

"Take my bike," he said solemnly. "You'll need serious ammo. I found these in our shed. There's nothing better."

Gary handed me a dusty bag full of marbles. Blood reels, cat's eyes, tom bowlers and a heavy-calibre ball bearing. What a bounty of materiel! I filled my pockets with the missiles while he assumed my position in the bushes. A renewed torrent of stones and insults distracted the enemy as I sneaked off. I rode past the Avalon to the bridge and crossed the creek. The bike was abandoned on the other side as I crept up the path through the reserve.

When I reached the ravine, I realised slaughter threatened at close range. The odds were three to one, but it was too late to go back, honour intact. I crawled to the edge of the bush, commando-style. The enemy position was unprotected from the rear. Surprise attack. I rushed out and fired a rapid volley at each invader. The boys howled in pain and abandoned the fort. They ran off protesting about unfair tactics. I kept firing. No prisoners!

I ascended the ravine and raised my arms in triumph to a chorus of cheers from the other side of the water. The conquerors soon arrived to bask in the spoils of war. But for me the excitement wore off quickly. Somehow, the victory had left a sense of anticlimax. What had we won? What good are warriors and weapons when there's no more foe? We reclaimed the golden ball, dismantled the enemy fort and planned a new hut. It was never built.

Thorry gathered up the slingshots left behind and wandered around the battleground looking for other booty.

"Hey, come and have a look at this!" he yelled.

We ran to join him in a hidden alcove at the other end of the bank. An abandoned bikini top lay in the sand next to an unopened packet of Trojans, a picnic rug and an empty bottle of Bacchus Reserve Hermitage. Someone obviously had a better time than firing rocks and insults across a creek. But it looked like a hurried departure for some reason. A large flat boulder stood nearby with seven candle stubs on top. Strange markings were drawn in the sand. I'm not sure what really happened. Perhaps one day I'll solve the mystery.

I looked around the boulder and caught a dull glint in a deep crack. Something had fallen deep inside. Maybe it was valuable. We took turns to reach through the jagged rocky edges that protected the treasure. Whatever was down there might be the key to the moonlight revelry, I thought. I plunged my hand into the crack, ignoring the cuts and scratches. I felt a metal object and pulled it out. The reward for my pains was an old, tarnished harmonica.

We were all disappointed with this find but agreed I'd won the right to keep it as a battle trophy. With a vague commitment to meet again the next day, we drifted off our separate ways. I returned home, dressed my cut hand, and examined the harp. It felt solid and powerful to hold. Was this the reward for my combat wounds?

If so, it deserved a clean-up. A rubdown with a rag and silver polish revealed a mysterious symbol etched on the top cover plate. Egyptian? The body was made of some alloy, embedded with tiny blue flecks. I blew it. The sound was piercing, but hardly musical. A slide button at one end doubled the range of notes, but also made the whole instrument more puzzling.

Restoration complete, I placed the harp next to Cerberus, my dog skull on the book shelf, and returned to reading comic books. For the first time, I noticed an advertisement on the back cover of *The Adventures of Odysseus*. The Apollo School of Music was offering correspondence lessons. A black-and-white drawing mimicked the familiar Charles Atlas bodybuilding courses.

The central figure was a harmonica player with a wreath on his head, surrounded by an adoring circle of long-robed females.

"Apollo Taught Orpheus. I'll Teach You!" said the heading. "Follow the Call to Adventure in music. Send coupon now for free trial offer."

The address was a post-office box in Canberra. My curiosity was aroused. I cut out the coupon along its Corinthian borders and sent it off. There was nothing better to do. I had lost interest in wars and weapons.

SEVEN STEPS TO HEAVEN

The following days, I checked the letterbox impatiently every few hours. The first correspondence lesson was shaped like an ancient Greek scroll, but the content was disappointing. It bore little relation to the saturnalian scenes my imagination had conjured by the creek. The introduction was cast in the lofty, archaic style reserved for wizards, arch-villains and tribal chieftains in matinee movies and radio serials.

> Greetings from afar. You have been chosen to undertake a musical journey. The Apollo School of Music will guide and protect you.

Chosen?

> The staff you wield on this pilgrimage is the chromatic harmonica. Mastery

of the instrument is a demanding
endeavour, but one that bestows
rewards on those who are dedicated.

What about the long-robed females?

Once known as the Aeolina, the
harmonica's ancestry can be traced
to the times men strode with gods.
One fabled instrument was forged
by a Chinese Qi master from a
meteorite. Some believe it was found
by Australian journalist George
Morrison, when Peking's palaces were
ransacked after the Boxer Rebellion.

Hmm. Not sure about all that. But I kept reading.

Assiduously practise the exercises
prescribed in these lessons and
follow their counsel.

The following pages included holding techniques,
an introduction to reading music and simple melodies.
Scattered throughout the book were physical exercises,
quaint homilies about personal conduct and even warnings about the lifestyle hazards of some musical journeys.

Such advice had all the appeal of the Year Eight pastoral assemblies at high school and the senior master's warnings against self-abuse. ("Can we stop when we need glasses, Sir?") I dismissed Apollo's homilies or skipped them. At first. After blowing myself dizzy, I grudgingly returned to the sections on proper breathing. Then the rest of it started to make sense.

The lessons included a quirky collection of folk songs, standards and lesser-known melodies. Swing Low Sweet Chariot progressed to Song of India, As Time Goes By and the complex Brazilian beat of Samba de Orfeu. A big challenge was to follow Wagner's Ride of the Valkyries into Valhalla, without it sounding like the schlocky music of a pinball game.

I worked my way through the books *assiduously* and completed the tests at the end of each correspondence lesson. These returned with a lyre stamp, handwritten corrections and encouraging comments. Sometimes, more homilies were included, such as: *Honour thy Muse*.

Despite my progress, I had to accept that the sound produced was often piteous. It would set Argos, the family dog, howling in unison if I left the bedroom door open. In a fit of pique one day, I attached an angry note to the completed lesson. The school's repertoire was *corny* and I *wouldn't be seen dead* playing any of it in public. I demanded to know if future lessons had *something better to offer*.

The same day, a thin parcel arrived. It contained an LP, a sheet of music and an unperturbed reply:

```
You are now ready to Cross the
Threshold. First, review the
section in Lesson 3 on Reaching the
Spheres. Then, listen to the enclosed
gramophone recording and learn the
scale on the accompanying sheet. It
will take you through a three-part
journey. Twelve bars later, you'll
return to the place you started,
ready to progress further.
```

I couldn't work this out, but checked the sheet. It contained just one line of seven notes: D, F, G, A♭, A, C, D. I played the scale. Big deal. Nothing remarkable there.

I placed the record on the turntable. Perhaps the ritual of vinyl worship would summon something significant: brush the polished diamond; lower the arm on the outer groove; close the plexiglass shell; wait in anticipation through the surface noise for the music to start.

Magic!

The LP featured Chicago blues players using the same scale up and down their harps. Bending and over-blowing the notes they produced an endless variety of riffs, runs and melodies: James Cotton; Sonny Boy Williamson; Junior Wells; Big Walter Horton and others. A pantheon of gods 'kissing tin.'

The raunchy sound sent shivers up and down my spine. The scale was my Seven Steps to Heaven. A musical koan of deceptive simplicity. I clapped with two hands.

I picked up my harp and played along with the Muddy Waters track, entering the world of gypsy fortune tellers, Lucky Sevens and voodoo charms. The two strongest beats in Hoochie Coochie Man were phantoms themselves. They appeared in the silence between repetitions of the haunting riff.

The dog stopped howling and started to bark.

I sent thanks to Apollo with a request for more blues lessons and recordings. The letter returned unopened and stamped *Not known at this address*. I tried a second letter. Same result. Directory Assistance had no record of the school. I felt lost and disappointed. My guide had abandoned me. I was on my own again.

"Where will I go from here, Apollo?"

If you believe Dr. Jung, there are no coincidences. The answer came quickly, announced by the notes D and A from the front doorbell. Thorry, Laszlo and Gary had called around to drag me off to the Saturday matinee.

"What are you doing Chris? Playing with yourself? Ho ho!"

"Haven't seen you since the Trojan War. Thought you were dead."

"There's a great flick on at the Olympus. It's about these bikers who take over a town."

"Come on, it starts at two."

After the usual fare of bland family movies, we thought *The Wild One* was really *cool*. For weeks afterwards we quoted Brando's lines and imitated his bored monotone.

"What are you rebelling against, Chris?"

"What have you got?"

Set in the white, pre-rock Fifties, the film's unusual soundtrack of bebop and big band mambo was more suited to beatniks than brawling, beer-drinking rebels. One bar scene showed a gang member jiving on a chromatic harp.

I recognised the run as a descending variation of the Seven Steps. I was also grabbed by the scene of Johnny the gang leader riding his Triumph at night. On the back sat Kathy, the small-town waitress and his saviour from nihilism.

Back home, I pulled out the lesson books again. They revealed further paths to explore. The Seven Steps helped me work out other scales and new melodies. Apollo had bestowed a gift. How to use it wisely was up to me.

Next time my friends came around, I was confident enough to play for them. Even the accomplished Laszlo. It started when Thorry looked through my bookshelf.

"You're still reading all that old stuff? It'll rot your brain. Haven't you got any Playboys?" He picked up the harp and blew it tunelessly to mock applause.

"You bled for this. Ever do anything with it?"

"Pass me my Excalibur, worthless vassal."

I hit them with a chorus of Juke Box Boogie. Their mouths fell open.

"Wow! Where'd you learn that?"

"I sold my soul at the crossroads, like Robert Johnson."

"I don't think the intersection of Kananook Street and McCulloch Avenue in Seaford has quite the ring of Highways 61 and 49 Clarksdale," said Laszlo.

It was my turn to be surprised.

"Very good! You'll know this then."

I clicked on the record-player. Johnson's haunting Hellhound on My Trail materialised through the scratches.

"Great song," said Gary. "Reminds me of your comic with those pictures of Cerberus guarding the gates of Hades."

"Great name for a group," added Laszlo.

We looked at each other.

"Do violinists make good guitarists?" I asked Laszlo.

"For sure. Just ask Paganini. According to the story, he cut the same deal to play like a master. They say he used strings made of human gut."

We were intrigued, but feigned disgust.

"I've also got a birthday coming up," said Laszlo.

The group took shape with a life of its own. Thorry's mad, hammering approach to the world made him a born drummer, while Gary's steadfast and solid nature suited the bass. Passing a pawnshop, Laszlo spotted a red Gibson SG, shaped like the Devil's horns. He talked his reluctant parents into buying it for him. That gave Thorry and Gary leverage to ask for instruments as well. HellHound was born. Spawned perhaps.

The first down payment came later.

▬▬▬▬▬▬▬

Only the Mentor Instant Study Guides helped us scrape through high school and university, as we spent most of our time practising or playing together. The music became our purpose and passion.

Music and motorbikes. Gary liked tinkering and had restored some old bikes with his father's help. Pride of place was an Indian Chief, favoured by World War II despatch riders.

For band transport we found an old black van going cheap. On its side, Thorry painted a fearsome three-headed dog surrounded by flames. Gary made the van more or less roadworthy and added a set of chariot-spoked mags. The image was completed when we rearranged the Johnson number as HellHound's theme song. It came together with a solid bass line, Thorry's rasping vocal, Laszlo's whiplash guitar and a blasting harp solo.

We launched the van at the Seaford crossroads, where I poured a bottle of cheap whisky over the bonnet.

"I dub thee the Black Argo. May all who sail with you boogie fearlessly."

"I can't wait for the groupies," said Thorry. "When do we get to christen it properly?"

That ceremony occurred on my birthday, the night of our first paid performance. HellHound had built up a following at school events, which led to a gig at the Youth Crusader Awards in a local church hall. The band's name created some problems for the social committee, but they needed a cheap crowd-puller.

Halfway through the evening the dancing stopped for the award presentations. During the long break I went to the van to change a faulty mike lead. The quiet car park was also an opportunity for a discreet swig from the hip-flask that was now standard issue for the group.

"Want to try something more exciting?" asked a voice in the dark.

Thorry's sister was waiting by the van. I was surprised to see her. Seldom had the friends of Helen's little brother been granted a show of interest by the blonde, blue-eyed winner of the Miss Mornington Peninsula Award.

"Hi, Helen. Where's King Menelaus?" I asked, using the ironic nickname for her imperious husband.

"Oh, playing war games I suspect, on one of his weekend military camps."

"I would have never expected to see you in the Blessed Oliver Plunket carpark."

She moved closer. Much closer.

"I didn't feel like a spartan night alone. Thought I'd catch the group. Sexy sound. You guys have a real future."

"It beats wars on the Kananook."

"You know, I never did get to thank you properly for defending my honour. A bit of a lost cause, though."

She brushed aside the hip-flask. The kiss was long, wet and passionate. Our tongues jousted furiously. We stopped to catch breath for another bout.

"Does this mean I get to carry your colours in battle?"

"Depends on the lance."

Her tight jeans rubbed against mine. We were getting to know each other.

"Mmm. But come and try something else, first."

"At your service."

We spread out the sleeping bags in the van and closed the door. She opened a packet of Drum, licked a few cigarette papers together and sprinkled the contents of an Alfoil sachet onto a twist of tobacco.

"What is it?"

"Sanjivani. A special herb from far away."

She rolled the large joint expertly, lit up and passed it to me.

"Big breaths."

"Yeth, I know."

"Cheeky young bugger."

A cloud of smoke enveloped us and Helen became the most beautiful woman in the world. The face that launched a thousand hips. The click of the belt buckles, the snap of the copper studs and the buzzing of the zips sounded simultaneously, like a well-drilled platoon presenting arms. We took up our positions. Both sides were exposed.

The windows steamed up. We continued until victory was almost mine to claim. Then she seized the tactical advantage.

"Not bad for a beginner. But you need practice."

"Touché. Mind if I use that line some day?"

"Have I ever denied you anything?"

We paused to regroup.

The joust climaxed with a crescendo of explosions and the earth moved. Or rather the van. Gary and Laszlo were rocking it as hard as they could. Thorry thumped the sides like bongos. A rhumba.

"So that's where you went."

"We wondered what was taking so long."

"Come on. It's show time."

"Happy birthday," said Helen.

She sat up and slipped on her jeans.

"I have to get back."

She opened the door.

"We'll always have Paris."

"Humphrey Bogart's or Homer's?"

"Hi, Sis," said Thorry, sniffing the air. "Menny's away again?"

She walked off without answering. I clambered out doing up my belt. The intruders dismissed my curses with knowing grins that grew broader when I threw up on the back mudguard. Thorry handed me a towel.

"Must have been the dope," he said.

"Must have been," I replied, wiping my mouth.

My playing was off the rest of the night. There had to be a better way.

▐▌▐▌▐▌▐▌

The word got out and the band gained notoriety. The van itself was an attraction when parked outside a venue, like the site of some ancient fertility ritual. We staged shock antics to bolster HellHound's rebel image. A marketing decision that appealed to the activist groups who sometimes booked us. Some of their politics rubbed off.

At a benefit for Rainforest Liberation one night, I blew burning lighter fluid through the harp at the end of a fiery solo, so to speak. Not to be outdone, Thorry dropped sticks, disappeared briefly and returned. Before we could stop him, he streaked across the stage wearing nothing but a dangling football sock for the Melbourne Demons team. Like Hanuman incarnate, a sheet of burning toilet paper trailed from his buttocks.

What symbolism!

The crowd loved it.

However, we soon agreed to drop the pyrotechnics. They distracted from our playing, the lighter fluid tasted terrible and Thorry couldn't sit down properly for a week after misjudging the burn rate of Kleenex two-ply. We also got warnings from the vice squad and fire department.

That concert was memorable for other reasons. An A&R man from Stentor Records approached us about cutting a disk. And it was the night Gary revealed he was getting married.

The announcement was no great surprise. Gary had dated Sibyl since high school. She was a quiet, contemplative vegetarian, who read fortunes with Egyptian tarot cards. The two shared something special at a time the rest of us found it hard to maintain relationships. Girlfriends tired of coming second to the music. I could understand that. Listening to scales practised for hours on end would drive anyone crazy.

"This calls for the best buck's night in history," said Thorry, when he heard the news. "And I know just the place. My son, it is fitting that your last night of freedom should be commemorated at the old bike track. Leave the organisation to me."

There wasn't much to organise. Just a lot of booze, a large bonfire and spreading the word to our circle of friends, musos and bikers. About thirty of us gathered around the fire in the amphitheatre-shaped paddock. The music broke out with the first round of drinks.

I was blowing along with Laszlo, Thorry and others when we heard the distinctive roar of The Sorcerer on his green Harley. Brujo looked like a flamenco player from Central Casting: gold ear-rings, black unkempt hair and a face almost as scarred as the battered Ramirez slung across his back. Two wives and ten years older than the rest of us, he was cynical about most things, including marriage. But the promise of live music and the prospect of some wild, macho fun, was an irresistible invitation.

Brujo got off his bike and swaggered over to greet us by the fire, guitar drawn. Thorry was beating out an Afro rhythm on a hollow log and a 44-gallon drum. Brujo sat next to him, took two long pulls on a flagon of rough red and started strumming along.

He warmed up to assume the savage and wandering anarchy of his forebears. Hands a blur, the rhythms and runs flew through Morocco, India, Greece, then back to Malaga. Brujo's impassioned singing recalled a thousand campfires and their stories.

We stopped our playing to watch him become trans-fixed in the spell of his *duende*. Upstaged by the magician, the fire crackled and threw out sparks in anger. Brujo could have gone on for hours, but one of the silver-bound strings finally snapped under the strain.

We cheered and poured another round of drinks. The Sorcerer upended his flagon again to signal he had re-joined us. Gary was standing to one side looking gloomy.

"What's up?" I asked. "It's your night."

"I don't want to seem ungrateful, but I had a big fight with Sibyl. She actually tried to stop me coming tonight. Said she had a bad feeling about it. She doesn't understand what all this means."

Brujo had overheard as he changed his guitar string. He laughed.

"My friend, she is a woman. She understands better than you think. She knows she must make you change your loyalties to be a good husband. To tie you down. Soon you must stay home at night. You'll sell your bike, buy a station wagon, push a motor-mower on weekends. She will..."

Gary recoiled and I broke in.

"Brujo, you're acting like a prick! This is supposed to be a celebration, not the Spanish Inquisition."

He stiffened, half rose and then smiled.

"You're right, Chris. I am a bad party guest. Gary, pay no attention to the drunken ravings of an aging bachelor, who's lost his head. Let's liven things up a bit."

He got up, slapped Gary on the back and yelled out to Thorry.

"That beat you were playing when I arrived. Play it again. Loudly! We owe Gary a lap of honour."

Thorry's beat rang out as Brujo rounded up all the riders. One by one the bikes awoke growling. We turned on our high beams and circled the fire. Brujo spun his Harley round, weaving in and out of the procession in the opposite direction. A ritual fire-dance for the gods to watch from above.

Brujo skidded to a halt in front of the fire and the others lined up beside him. One by one the brutes were quietened. Thorry kept hammering the drum. Brujo chanted Gary's name in time to the beat and we joined in, responding to each repeated call. The chant continued until it was time for another drink.

Gary perked up. He had forgotten Brujo's words. We thought.

"Thanks for the tribute. Now it's my turn to give you something to talk about around the campfire before I supposedly get grounded."

He strode over to his bike.

"What are you going to do, Gary?" asked Laszlo.

"Fly over the flames. Escape suburbia."

"Don't be a mad bastard," I said. "You're pissed."

"Not that pissed. Besides, I've done it before."

That was true. The fire was set against a rise in the paddock that formed a natural ramp. The jump was one of his favourite stunts. But that was sober, in daylight, without a fire.

Now, as the centre of attention, he didn't want to lose face. My arguments only strengthened his determination. I grabbed his arm, but there was no holding him back. Gary broke free, ran to his bike and kick-started it.

The metal beast reared up on its back wheel. He flicked on the light and raced to the end of the paddock. Gary stopped, turned and lined up the rise. Gunning his motor furiously, he sped towards the fire. The bike hit the rise in top gear and took off, clearing the flames.

"You're going too high!" I called.

The headlight cut an arc in the sky like a falling comet. The bike flipped and crashed hard with Gary underneath.

We ran over. His face, pale in the firelight looked up in shock. We carefully removed the wrecked bike, its front wheel still spinning. Gary's legs had been crushed. A strange burnt smell permeated the air, but there was no sign he'd be born anew. I grasped a cold, shaking hand. As he turned his head towards me.

"You flew, Gary. You flew. More than halfway to heaven."

Brujo rode off for an ambulance. The fire died down.

Gary and Sibyl's wedding was a bedside ceremony in the hospital. He was still in traction when their son was born.

A JOURNEY TO THE WEST

The shock, guilt and sorrow hit me all at once.

"I should've tackled him harder, before he got on the bike."

"You couldn't do that to a mate," said Thorry. "He'd done it before."

"There was no stopping him. He had something to prove," said Laszlo

The solid bass heartbeat was gone. Gary had always been the calm, steadying voice. The one who thought everything through methodically and kept the group mobile, in more ways than one. But Brujo's words had found their way through a chink in reason's armour.

The fall also forced us to face the truth that we were mortal. Brujo disappeared after that night. Rumours said he died in a motorbike accident or drank himself to death. Or both.

HellHound never made the record. The company offered us a session player but we refused. It would have felt like a betrayal. Rehearsals became visits to the rehab ward. In turn, these sessions became a ritual of forced bonhomie and banter. Gary tried joining in, but mostly lay there helpless amongst the wires and weights, as if trussed up in Vulcan's chains.

The next visit, I noticed two teenagers sleeping in beds across the room, with battered wheelchairs chained to them.

"What's going on there?"

"I call them Achilles and Damian. They're also paras, sleeping off the tranqs the nurses gave them. You might remember them from the shanghai war. We're mates now."

"Why the chains?"

"They broke out of here on those chairs and knocked off their doctor's Jag from the carpark. Acka steered and shifted the gearstick, while Damy lay on the floor working the pedals. The cops freaked when they pulled them over near Seaford. Two escapees from the spinal unit with floppy legs, wearing blue hospital gowns."

"I guess old habits die hard," said Laszlo. "But what a triumph of the will."

After a long silence, I asked the inevitable question.

"Well, what do *we* do now? Get day jobs or start playing again?"

Which really meant: "We can't go on like this, but we don't want Gary to think we're abandoning him."

Thorry and Laszlo looked at me, not knowing what to say. Sibyl turned to us. Her eyes, no longer red-rimmed, had regained their far-seeing look.

"Why not do both? Work your way round Australia? You used to talk about touring. Start with a journey to the West. There's lots of labouring jobs over there and you could play at night. They're starved of entertainment in those small towns."

The call sounded rehearsed. It was hard to work out whether she'd come up with a realistic solution or was just trying to get rid of us. But whatever Sibyl's motive, we knew it was time to break out in our own way.

"My brother made a fortune at the Corazon gold-mine in the Northern Territory," she said. "You could come back and set up something for all of us. Our own recording studio, perhaps. Just for blues."

"We can't tour without our bass," said Laszlo. "Besides, carting all that equipment across Australia in an old van wouldn't work."

"You can survive without bass," broke in Gary. "We can't spend the rest of our lives just sitting around looking at each other."

He assumed his serious, practical tone. "You can play without the amps and all the other gear. Go unplugged. Harp, cut-down drum-kit and acoustic guitar. Take the

12-string. It fills the room and most places have a PA system of sorts. Just like the old delta bluesmen in the juke joints. Back to where it all began."

That was the first positive mood since the buck's night. It felt right. Thorry tapped a beat on the table and tried to channel the voice of Big Bill Broonzy.

> *I got the key to the highway, billed out and bound*
> > *to go.*
> *I'm gonna leave here runnin', because walkin' is most*
> > *too slow.*

The rest of the visit turned into an animated discussion about repertoire, equipping the van and when to 'start runnin.' Sibyl said the night of a full moon was a good time to set off on a voyage. That gave us three weeks.

"Fellers, just two favours," said Gary as we left the ward. "Lots of postcards. And paint over the monster on the Argo. We did enough of that stuff."

The rest of the month flew by as we packed up, stored boxes of records and farmed out dogs. Even Thorry's snow-dome collection found a home. Sometimes you have to choose between kitsch and the Road.

The round of farewell parties included a poolside send-off hosted by The Three Sisters on departure night. Calling themselves Morgan, Calypso and Rati, the trio of singing sirens sometimes joined us on stage. They'd previously refused offers of even closer collaboration ventures and it seemed a pity they had finally summoned us, just when we were leaving.

The Three Sisters shared a house in the Dandenong Ranges, just outside Melbourne. We agreed to meet there for a farewell party. Thorry was to pick up Laszlo after fitting a roo-bar to the van, while I wanted one last ride on my bike before storing it.

The evening was warm and Arion seemed to know the way. The full moon followed me along the narrow winding road up through the forest. A secluded property with a high fence stood by a river. The sign said *Kangra—Valley of Love*. I turned in. A wrought-iron gate with a boomerang crest opened by itself. Burning torches lined a long driveway leading to a large house with white stuccoed walls. Surrounded by cypress pines, it looked like a Spanish mission with a multi-coloured roof of curved terracotta tiles. I parked my bike near the front door, where a screeching peacock announced my arrival.

Calypso and Rati were setting a table by the pool and greeted me with their captivating smiles. I walked down the path towards them. Patchouli and sandalwood incense scented the air. The pool curved sensuously through a sheltered grove with a pink, lotus-shaped fountain in the middle.

"Fantastic place you have here."

"A little piece of paradise," replied Rati. "Our guests usually want to stay on."

Morgan walked out of the house and joined us.

"Laszlo just phoned. They're not coming. Thorry went to one farewell too many this afternoon and got picked up. He's sleeping it off in custody, so you can't leave until tomorrow."

"Did Laszlo say what happened?" I asked

"It seems a patrol car found a black van driving slowly down the road with its left-hand wheels scraping the gutters. Thorry argued that he was being responsible because he knew he was too drunk to drive in a straight line unassisted."

"Typical Thorry," I groaned, while the others laughed.

"So, it looks like we've got you all to ourselves," said Calypso, with a hint of mischief.

"You must need a drink after coming all the way up here. Care to try the house cocktail? Pure ambrosia!"

"And you must have one of our manna muffins," added Morgan. "Definitely not from a White Wings packet. And we don't want you to starve to death."

I tried both. The drink was sweet, with a hint of rosewater and something else. The muffins were shaped like small cupolas and tasted of cinnamon. A large hammock beckoned. The perfect place for us to lie together and sway by the water. A floating sensation came over me with the soft, rhythmic movement.

"Is that a harp in your pocket, or are you just happy to see us?" quipped Cal.

I pulled it out and blew some languorous runs in time to the swaying. The polished silver caught the moonlight and the engraved symbol lit up. Rati looked over.

"I've always meant to ask you. What is that sign?"

"Looks Celtic," said Morgan.

"Or ancient Greek," suggested Calypso.

I turned the harp over in my hand.

"It seems to come from everywhere. Depending on which way you look at it. Laszlo thinks it's Romany and an African muso said it was Yoruban. The mark of Xango, the god of lightning and thunder."

Cal climbed out of the hammock.

"Time for a swim"

"Play something special for us?" said Rati.

"Not blues for a change. Music for apsaras to bathe by."

She slid out of her clothes and walked down the steps into the pool. The others did the same. I almost dropped the harp at the sight of their pure white bodies in the water. They splashed each other, laughing. The drops of water fell in slow motion, leaving milky traces in the air.

What to play on an occasion like this?

A long-forgotten melody from the correspondence lessons stirred in my memory: Song of India, a 1930s big band standard 'adapted' from a Rimsky-Korsakov opera.

"Not so corny after all," I could hear Apollo saying.

I played it slowly, wrapping my heart around the yearning notes. I watched them drift across the water and caress The Three Sisters. They stopped swimming, waded to the marble edge and sang along in a heavenly three-part harmony. They swayed to the melody like a snake charmer's flute.

The grove was silent when we finished. Then came alive with swirls of colour. A golden deer walked by. It stopped to eat a ripe pear from one of the fruit-laden trees.

"Well played, Hylas," said Calypso. "You may join the nymphs."

I stripped and dived in. The water made my body tingle all over, like a thousand tiny kisses.

Rati swam to the shallow end and stood up. A silhouette of divine nakedness reached towards to the sky, grasped the moon and pulled it into the water. She threw the large white ball at Morgan.

"Come on, Chris! Keepings-off. Try to take it from us."

We were now children playing in the dawn of the world. Laughing, falling, splashing, touching. Calypso bent over the ball and clasped it to her breasts. I leant over, grabbed her from behind and felt her pressing against me.

Rati came to the rescue. She wrapped her arms around my waist and blew a raspberry on my lower back, sending a charge up the spine.

"Bullseye. Right on the chakra," she laughed. "Let's see what that does to your kundalini."

It was too much. I let Calypso go as I felt the coiled serpent stirring. The worm that would despoil Eden's innocence. Luckily the water was waist deep. I restricted my movements lest the shameful, wanton serpent be detected.

"Do you really have to go tomorrow? Why not stay?" they chorused

The temptation was strong. What a life we could have here! I thought about it for a while, but I realised I was committed to the odyssey. The night was special, but it wouldn't last.

"I'd love to but... I'm tied up."

They exchanged glances.

"We're disappointed," said Morgan.

The game quietened down.

"We're getting cold," said Calypso.

They climbed out of the pool and dressed.

"Are you coming out?"

I was turning Krishna-like blue but pretended I wanted to swim a bit longer.

The headlights of a car swept the drive. Two crystal eyes cast the harsh beams of reality, like a waiter turning up with the bill for forbidden fruit. Credit cards not accepted.

"It's Mother," said Morgan.

Mother?

A tall woman dressed in black got out of a Firebird and walked over to the pool. I was introduced and said hello, limply.

"I thought I'd drop by on the way home and make sure you were behaving yourselves," joked Mrs. Mara.

"How was the opera?" asked Rati.

"Oh, splendid. They don't often perform Sadko these days. He was quite a minstrel!"

She saw me shiver.

"You must be freezing. Why not join us for a hot chocolate?"

Aware of my nakedness, I remembered my clothes were on the chair next to her.

"It's, er, stimulating here. I'd like to stay a bit longer."

"We'll wait for you."

Okay, let's see if the seventies have really hit the hills.

I climbed out of the pool, dried myself very casually by the chair and put my clothes on. Mrs. Mara drew a short breath when she noticed my state, then carried on talking about the performance.

"I particularly enjoyed the frenzied court revels in the Sea-King's domain."

The Three Sisters grinned.

I finished dressing and slipped the harp back into my pocket.

46

"Interesting symbol," said Mrs. Mara. "One of the marks that Buddha was born with, if I'm not mistaken."

She looked through me.

"Perhaps it will protect you as well."

"As long as you don't turn me into a stag."

The peacock screeched.

"I think I'll skip the chocolate, if you don't mind," I said. "It's getting late and we're supposed to leave early."

We said good-bye with chaste cheek kisses.

"Are you sure you won't stay?" said a wistful Rati. I started the bike and kicked it into first gear. The back wheel pawed the ground impatiently.

"Catch you next time," yelled Morgan in the distance as I left the driveway and descended.

<hr>

We reached the border late afternoon and crossed the river. Thorry complained the whole way about his thumping head and cancelled licence. Laszlo drove in sullen silence. He was peeved about bailing out Thorry, instead of enjoying a brief glimpse of Paradise. My scant, censored account of events only added to the conviction he'd missed out. He drove without a break to emphasise his martyrdom.

I was working through my own feelings of sadness, longing, uncertainty. What was I doing in a rattly van with a grumpy guitarist and a self-pitying drummer?

But by the time we reached the desert, the rhythm of the road had worked its magic. Cleansing the past and promising the excitement of an unknown future. Thorry was asleep, snorting irregularly.

"Typical drummer," I said to Laszlo. "Can't even snore in time."

He looked sideways at me and we both laughed.

The romance of the open highway lasted only a few days, until we hit the unmade section of the Nullarbor Plain. During a pit stop, Thorry noticed leaking drops of oil on the road.

"It's the differential. The gasket's gone."

"God knows where we'll find another one out here," said Laszlo

"The diff'll seize if we keep going," Thorry added, unnecessarily.

"What would Gary do?' asked Laszlo.

I shook the dust from my head.

"I remember him telling me once how it happened to him. He cut a gasket out of a Corn Flakes packet. It formed a good enough seal to keep him going."

We emptied the food box. No cereal boxes, just muesli in recyclable plastic bags and Thorry's tinned spaghetti.

"Trust my luck to be stuck in the desert with two health freaks," he complained. "Why can't you eat crap for breakfast like everyone else?"

"That *canned* crap isn't going to help us either," Laszlo snarled back. "Men of darkness eat food which is stale and tasteless."

"Come on you two! We won't get anywhere like this. Let's have another look."

We unloaded the van on the side of the road, but could find nothing suitable. The sun blazed. I passed around the canvas water bag hanging on the front bumper. The desert shimmered into infinity on all sides. We hadn't seen another car all day.

"We might as well pack all the gear back in the van and wait," said Laszlo.

He picked up the toolbox and jumped. A black-headed snake slithered out of my canvas army-bag into the scrub. I picked up the bag and shook it at arm's length to check for other visitations. An old lesson-book fell out. Solutions to Common Problems, said the gasket-sized cardboard cover—about the thickness of a Corn Flakes packet. Thank you again, Apollo.

It took three hours to jack up the van, remove the differential, cut and fit the makeshift gasket. The seal held enough oil to reach the next town, a hundred miles on.

Walpurgis was built around a railway siding and a coven of thirteen wheat silos. It looked pretty dead. We found a garage and woke the mechanic, asleep on an old car seat. He replaced the gasket, still yawning, and went back to sleep when he'd finished. We made for the nearest pub, looking forward to showers and a bed, instead of a grimy sleeping-bag by the side of the road.

But the first priority was a cold beer in the downstairs bar of the Terminus Hotel. The dark old pub leant over the railway track, as if exhausted by the heat. The iron roof a rusty mantle, with rotten veranda posts as caryatids.

Inside, the place was nearly empty. A race call droned from a radio-cassette player held together with insulating tape. I sat on the corner stool by the faded photo of a dejected local football team. A beer jug containing water and a floating fishing-bob stood on the bar by my elbow. A light-gauge line, tied to the bob, extended upwards through a crack in the ceiling.

"What's that for?" I asked Samuel the barman as he handed me a beer. He looked wistful.

"The other end of the line goes through the ceiling to the bed-springs of the Honeymoon Suite, just above us. If newlyweds had booked the room in the old days, we'd gather round the jug and check out their performance over a few schooners."

"Did anyone keep the records?"

Samuel shrugged his shoulders.

"There's not much to do in this town. It kept the drinkers here for hours, discussing form and betting on repeat bouts. But that's gone now, since Sergeant Yama moved in and took over."

"Who's he?"

"Yama's the new cop they sent from the east after some reports about the way we do things around here. That one-eyed wowser jumps on any fun and thumps the shit out of anyone who complains."

Samuel pointed to his broken nose and missing tooth. Thorry seized the opportunity to turn the conversation our way.

"Sounds like you could do with some entertainment. Let me tell you about HellHound." He pointed to the radio-cassette. "Does that thing still work?"

Thorry inserted the band's demo tape and played the first track. Samuel was interested.

"It's what we need tonight! There's a road gang passing through and they'll be looking for a good time. I'll call the boss."

The publican gave us the go-ahead and worked out a door-deal for our performance. Thorry looked the barroom up and down.

"Unplugged be buggered. We'll have to find a PA system!"

"I just happen to have my harp mike," I said.

Laszlo opened his shoulder bag and pulled out a clip-on guitar pickup.

"I also brought this, just in case."

"We've got work to do."

Samuel helped us track down an amplifier and speakers, used for meetings by the Country Women's Association. He rang all his mates to spread the word. By eight, the bar was noisy with truckers, road workers and locals. Expectations were high. HellHound held a council-of-war.

"Nothing fancy, lots of boogie and push it hard," I said. "They'll know On the Road Again, so we start with that."

After a quick and dirty sound check, I introduced the group and we launched straight into the opening riff of the first song. A roar of approval applauded the choice. Laszlo's 12-string pumped out a rhythm of full barre-chords to Thorry's pounding beat. The stamping Blundstone boots raised dust from the old floorboards. A raucous male chorus joined us on the hook-line. Samuel turned up the volume.

Jailhouse Blues followed and HellHound kept the heat up for the whole set. Thorry was in great voice. We blew out our pains, sorrows and frustrations. No catharsis like the blues. After almost a full hour we stopped for a drink. Laszlo and I joined the crowd at the bar, throwing down the beers they shoved at us. Thorry stayed behind with his drum kit to adjust an overworked snare.

The room hushed as the biggest cop I'd ever seen walked down the stairs. An angry Cyclops of a man. Obviously not a music lover! Thorry had fixed his snare and replaced the drum. To test it, he accompanied Sergeant Yama's ominous entrance with a circus drum-roll and cymbal clash. Bloody drummers! Even their social timing's off.

The drinkers groaned. Sergeant Yama was not impressed. He marched over to the fount of his irritation.

"Listen to that. A smartass!"

He faced Thorry closely.

"And a smartass from who-knows-where. We don't like the look of you around here."

Thorry twirled his sticks as if nothing had happened.

"I think you'll have to come with me," said Yama in a tone of false jollity.

"Oh, come on, Sergeant, where's your sense of humour?" said one of the drinkers.

"He was just having a bit of fun," added another. "This is not an SS rally."

Yama's voice turned menacing.

"I've got a Disturbing the Peace and an Offensive Behaviour here. Care to join him? Who knows? We might even have a Resisting Arrest."

Everyone slunk back. Yama grabbed Thorry's red hair and dragged him to the paddy wagon parked outside. I followed them. The Sergeant backhanded Thorry viciously, punched his stomach and threw him in the back.

"That should quieten you down a bit."

I heard Thorry retching as the paddy wagon drove off. I strode back inside. Laszlo could see what was coming. I shrugged off his attempts to calm me down. The PA was still switched on.

"What sort of place is this? You can't even have a drink and listen to a bit of music because of one cop. Are you his sheep? Or just so gutless that you're only capable of wanking yourselves around a beer-jug?"

I'd gone too far. Beer glasses slammed down and stools scraped the floor. Samuel broke in to redirect the anger.

"He's right. We've put up with it long enough."

He eyed some individuals in the crowd.

"Perhaps a few gentlemen who've enjoyed Sergeant Yama's hospitality should visit the station and persuade him to take a ride on tonight's wheat train."

Nodding heads showed he had a quorum. He leant over the bar and whispered to me conspiratorially.

"I've been waiting for this. There's a tow-chain in the back of my ute. Get your mate out and keep heading west. Sergeant Yama's going east and I don't think he'll be back."

Laszlo and I packed the instruments in the van. I found the chain, threw it in the front and started up. Laszlo grabbed me through the open window.

"Are you serious?"

"Look, Thorry could get three months if they add tonight's charges to last week's adventures. You don't have to come."

Laszlo paused. He walked to the passenger-door and climbed in.

"The bastard's mad. But he'd do it for me."

"You know if we go through with this, there's no going back."

Laszlo ignored the warning. "The cop shop's just off the main street, under the carobs near the post office. We passed it when we picked up the PA."

The lockup was a wooden shed behind the police station. I backed the van quietly up a nearby laneway. Laszlo crept to a barred window to alert Thorry. I bolted the chain round the rear axle and looped it through the bars of the door. The sole occupant grinned out with a bruised and bloodied face.

I drove forward, riding the clutch. The lockup was stronger than it looked and the wheels spun, whining, as we tried to wrench it open. The back door of the station opened, revealing the giant form of Sergeant Yama. We were trapped.

"What the fuck do you think you're doing?"

He stepped off the porch towards us, truncheon drawn.

Five men stepped from under the shadow of the carob trees. The outside light was smashed and the yard went dark.

The first fist found its mark with a loud smack. "How does it feel Sergeant?" said a familiar voice.

I backed up and drove forward again, foot flat. This time, the whole wooden wall came off in splinters and dragged in the dirt behind us. Thorry scrambled out and dived into the van. We unhooked the chain and sped away, high on fear and adrenaline. I kept the headlights off until the dark form of Walpurgis faded into the desert.

Thorry was the first to speak.

"Er... I guess I'll have to work on my drum-roll."

THE DEAD HEART

The Corazon mine was three days' hard driving north, into the heart of Australia. We shared the wheel in shifts and stopped only for gas, for fear of getting caught. As it turned out there was no need to worry. A local newspaper I picked up in a garage shop reported that Sergeant Cedric Yama would be transferred to head office after leaving hospital.

Cedric? The God of Death was named after a nondescript family sedan and Little Lord Fauntleroy?

The Desert Star told the story between the lines.

> During the typically vigorous execution of his duties, Sergeant Yama fell into an open freight car while investigating suspicious movements at the Walpurgis railway siding. He was found injured and unconscious. No witnesses to the accident have come forward.

"Serves the bastard right," said Thorry, stroking his bruised face.

"What about a record of the arrest and our modifications to the lockup?" asked Laszlo.

I flicked through the paper and saw a short notice in the Community Events section.

"Have a look. I think it'll be okay."

> Bartender, Samuel Peterson, is organizing a volunteer group to repair the exterior wall of the historic Walpurgis police station.
>
> "It apparently collapsed because of white ant infestation and needs to be fixed soon," he told the Star. "A willy willy has already blown away all the files lying around inside."

Three hours from the main road, Corazon looked like the set of a post-holocaust movie. Rows of ramshackle wooden huts and sheds with corrugated iron roofs littered the ravaged landscape. Old machinery and car bodies baked in the sun. Broken beer bottles scattered around the area glittered like thousands of coloured diamonds.

A creaky cable tower straddled a mine shaft, like a giant spider. It raised and lowered a cage repeatedly, as if it hoped something better would come up next time. Rusty carriages on a small railway fed ore to a noisy crushing mill that set our teeth on edge. Green oxide competed with the red dust to cover every surface.

A group of green wraiths stooped by a cairn of ore and shovelled it into bags.

"So, this is where we make our fortune," said Laszlo. "This place is straight out of the Egyptian Book of the Dead."

We found the manager's office in a pre-fab hut guarded by a cyclone wire fence. A crackly intercom demanded we state our business. An electric gate buzzed open before we could finish. Presiding over the office was a round, owlish figure in a transparent polyester shirt that revealed a mesh singlet underneath. Ossie held court with his hands crossed over his breast.

"Yes, we can always use some laborers. We have quite a turnover. You're not on the run are you? Heh, heh, just joking. We get all types here."

He ran an appreciative eye over Laszlo and opened a large ledger.

"You work your way up to being a miner. That's where the good money starts. Or you might even join the baggers who go off salary and get paid instead for each bag they fill. The price of copper's been rising, so they're doing extra well."

"Copper. No gold?" I asked.

"Gold?" he laughed again. "The alluvial deposit ran out ages ago. We manage to filter out only a few pennyweights to the ton these days."

"So, this is where we make our fortune," repeated Thorry.

Ossie chuckled. "Go west and find gold, eh? Well, there's plenty of overtime and double time on Sundays. If you work hard and don't piss or gamble it away, you'll end up with a bit."

Ossie slapped an air conditioner back to life and warmed to his narrative.

"I can remember only one bloke here who made what you'd call a fortune. An Easterner who cleaned up on the crap tables. They reckon he could predict the roll of the dice. The mob running the game soon got sick of it. After he'd won big, third night running, they went around to his hut to sort him out. But he'd cleared out. Seems he predicted their visit too."

"Sibyl forgot to tell us that part," said Laszlo.

"We're here now," I replied. "We'll have to make the most of it. There's nothing left in the kitty."

Ossie signed us on and handed over two keys.

"Your huts are in the last row. It's a bit quieter there. I herd all the drunks and desperates to the other end. Saves on repairs."

He looked at his watch. "You might as well have some lunch before moving in. Canteen's behind me."

He winked at Laszlo. "Come and see me if you have any other questions."

We left the office and walked quietly over to a long shed. On the way, we passed a miner tending a nasty wound on the side of his chest. He looked up at us.

"You blokes look new here. Be careful of cuts. They don't heal real well in this place."

The canteen had the weathered, distressed look adopted by inner-suburban jeans shops to look rugged and authentic. A sign on the door prohibited fighting, swearing or throwing food at the cooks. We soon found out why.

Rowdy groups of men in work shorts and faded blue singlets attacked their food at trestle tables. One got up and slammed his plate on the serving counter, complaining that his corned beef was off. Another miner passed a dessert around to his amused friends and pointed to a large blowfly perfectly preserved in the jelly.

We joined the food queue under a slowly spinning ceiling fan, spattered with the flies that had escaped the jelly. I felt a tap on my shoulder and turned to face one of the wraiths we'd seen earlier. Underneath the green dust was a dark, wiry man.

"I'm Theo. You mind telling me what's on the blackboard today? I don't read so good."

I went through the *Dailey Specialls* aloud and Theo invited us to eat with him. Twelve hours of bagging in silence each day made him an outgoing luncheon companion.

"I been here ten years now. Nowhere else someone like me get the same money. I can do one hundred bags a day. Soon I have enough to go back to my village and buy a farm. You heard of Lesbos?"

"Where Orpheus ended up?" I answered.

Theo was delighted not to hear the usual comment about his Aegean Island.

"Part of him. After the wild women tear him up, his head and lyre washed up near my village, Mythinma. I saw his ghost when I was little."

He spotted the slide button of my harp poking out of the pocket of my denim jacket.

"You play too. I can tell you boys don't belong here. Be careful. People come here to make money for a dream. They forget the dream, drink, gamble, stay for nothing. No past, no future. Look at them."

A group of Ossie's *desperates* shuffled into the canteen and poured themselves black coffee. Hungover, unshaven, they sat down at a corner table. One put his head between his hands.

"He get too drunk last night and lose everything. Five years' saving," whispered Theo. "His mates stop him shooting himself."

We sawed our way through the steaks, skipped dessert and finished off with tea from chipped enamel mugs. Theo showed us to our huts and returned to work.

"Great place," said Thorry, looking at the wire-mesh stretchers in the one-roomed hut.

He and I shared one hut. Laszlo chose to bunk alone next door. Before moving our stuff in, we had to clean up the bottles and other rubbish left behind. Under my bed, I found an old pewter goblet, green with age. Not quite the Holy Grail.

"Must have been someone's twenty-first," said Thorry, placing it on the shelf next to other treasures collected along the way. He missed his snow-domes.

Life soon became a routine of long, hot days shovelling up ore-bearing mud that spilled from the crushers, and building walls for the tailings dam. At night we were too tired to do anything but collapse on our beds.

But lying still for once had its rewards, such as watching the spectacular sunsets. In the semiconscious trance of exhaustion came the vision of Ra descending. A fiery orb that bled life into the dead heart's red soil.

Sometimes the breeze carried the faint sound of didgeridoo and clapstick from an Aboriginal settlement up the track. Theo said the people there described Corazon as a wound in their land. He claimed you could hear moaning noises whenever new shafts were sunk.

Around nine each night the drunken brawling broke out at the other end of the camp. A symphony of swearing, smashing glass and slamming doors. It lasted about an hour and we'd get to sleep by ten. We tried the makeshift casino a couple of times, but there were no fortunes to be made there. The odds were stacked against the players. Unless, of course, they could predict the fall of the dice.

Time passed. We became fitter and more used to the heavy work. One evening, after sunset, I started blowing my harp for the first time since our arrival at Corazon. I couldn't place the melody. It sounded like some music of the desert I must have heard ages before. Laszlo walked in with his guitar.

"Funny, I was thinking of the same thing. Must be the desert and the wild camels we saw. Have a listen to this arabesque tuning I've been trying out."

Laszlo had re-tuned the treble strings to make them sound like an oud. The basses were set up to produce a constant hypnotic droning while he played melody.

Thorry got up, grabbed his sticks and assembled his junk collection. Car parts, pieces of metal and old containers became bells, chimes and drums. He laid down an Ayoub rhythm.

Another instrument cut its way through the night like a curved dagger. The sound of hashish, heartache and sweet black coffee. It was Theo, sitting outside the hut, with a very battered bouzouki.

"I been listening to you for a while."

"Come on in!"

He ripped open a carton of stubbies and handed them out.

"I show you some rembetika my father teach me."

Theo's songs led us through a world of refugees and shanty towns from Piraeus to Istanbul, through Cairo and over to Jeddah. He nodded at us to keep the rhythm going and improvised wildly. His roughened fingers danced up and down the long, slender neck. Then he slowed the pace and quietened us down.

"Listen."

The music from a distant settlement was faint, but the sounds merged with ours to make one.

"We all play the same song," said Theo.

The music continued until some drunks staggered by and threw bottles on the roof.

"Australia for Australians!" they yelled. Theo ignored them.

"You boys play good. My cousin runs a place in Melbourne. You should see him when you get back. He's Cretan, but it doesn't matter."

"Theo, I don't know what you were singing," I said. "But it makes me feel like moving again. I miss the sea."

Thorry and Laszlo nodded in agreement.

"Ah, you understand rembetika. It's about missing people and places."

He put down the bouzouki and reached for his drink.

"Maybe it's time for you to go."

He looked around with a dismissive wave. "Not much more to learn here. Your penance is finished. I hear there's work in the Fremantle dockyards. Nice place, Perth."

It didn't take much convincing. We finished the stubbies and Theo stood up to leave.

"See you in Lesbos. Watch out for the wild women."

We got paid out the next day and packed the van.

"I didn't think you'd last this long," said Ossie. He looked with longing at Laszlo again. "Pity you're going."

The van barely made it to the coast. We lost second gear, the radiator leaked and only fencing wire held the engine in place when the mountings gave way. Heat, dust and constant repairs were getting monotonous. The dream was fading. But four days later our spirits revived, splashing in the Indian Ocean and drinking cappuccinos in sidewalk cafes.

Theo was right. A Texas-based company called Golden Petroleum needed dockyard laborers to paint and outfit a boat for oil surveying. Named after the God of Iron, the *Ogun* was a 100-foot trawler we found while wandering around the wharf.

Standing nearby with a clipboard was a tall, solid Texan, with a shock of red hair that made him look like a blazing pillar. His teeth were stained yellow from constant smoking.

"The name's Nat Sever," drawled the foreman, shaking our hands. "No, that's not from Nataraja Shiva, but it pays to worship me on the job."

"There's a month's work right here in Free-mantle. And if y'all shape up we'll keep you on as survey crew. We got shoots all the way from northwest Australia to the Gulf. Including India."

This was more like it. We signed on eagerly. The van had finally died and was sold to a scrapyard. RIP Styx ferry. We asked around for lodgings within walking distance of the shipyard. A ship's welder pointed to an old sandstone building near the waterfront. The Fremantle Sailor's Hostel. Flickering neon lights showcased the bleak, musty interior, with its worn-out lino floor. But it was cheap, convenient and would do for the month.

Laszlo was not convinced.

"We just seem to score one shit-hole after another. How many people have to spend their lives in places like this?"

We checked in anyway and that night went to the *Recreation Lounge* for a game of snooker. The table was torn and useless. A solitary old man had dozed off on the vinyl couch by a black-and-white Admiral TV screening Adventures in Paradise.

"Is that us in a few years?" said Laszlo. "Someone must think it is. Look at this."

He turned over the receipt for the first week's accommodation. The back showed a briefly-worded will bequeathing all property and worldly goods to the City of Fremantle Hostel for Sailors. Thorry saw the funny side of it.

"You've got some old rummy about to croak in an Aden bloodhouse. All he has to do is sign that receipt with his shaking hand and this place inherits his spyglass, wooden leg and swearing parrot."

He screeched and flapped his arms.

"They've obviously done very well with that one," I said. "You can see they've ploughed a lot of doubloons back into the decor."

We all laughed and went out for a bite to eat.

Outfitting the *Ogun* was better than shovelling mud in the desert. We painted the converted vessel and helped set up the survey equipment. The final touch was a large windlass holding more than a mile of hydrophone cable, bolted on the stern deck.

"Those four propane guns we installed yesterday go boom underwater," said Nat. "The sound waves bounce off the ocean floor. The streamer picks 'em up and the computer looks for hot spots."

The trickiest job was loading and storing the explosive gas containers.

"Don't drop those mothers!" Nat yelled as we struggled with the heavy steel bottles.

The metal hull had the superb acoustics of a cathedral. I practised harp some lunchtimes inside the large fuel tank, where the notes would resonate for ages and drift into the rest of the vessel. Nat was amused.

"Waal, seeing you like it so much in there, I've got a little job for you up in the bow. The chain locker needs to be painted with that goop."

He pointed to a heavy-duty brush and an evil-smelling container of thick black liquid. I climbed down a ladder into the depths of the locker and started slapping on the mixture. The vapour was strong in the enclosed space. Stronger than I realised.

I was suddenly fascinated by the extension light. The globe changed into a shaven head with a pointed beard. It grew horns. I smashed the light and blood spattered everywhere.

Darkness.

I was drifting at sea in an open boat and saw my missing father walking on the shore. I tried paddling towards him, but the current carried me away. A beautiful woman with long, dark hair emerged from the waves. She pointed to two paths that converged on the shore. One led to my faraway home, the other disappeared up a mountain. The current turned and the boat drifted towards the beach. I got out and walked up the steep, narrow path.

Thorry and Laszlo were looking at me anxiously when I woke up in the first aid room. Nat walked in and leaned over.

"You'll be okay. Sorry I forgot to tell you 'bout the mask you're supposed to wear. But it looks like you've earned your trip to the Pirate Coast. And your friends too, if they're interested."

They weren't. They were tired of searching for gold and wanted to return home. We shared our last dinner together that night. Laszlo had decided to go back and continue his music studies. Thorry was homesick for his family, his dog and his collections. He stroked his face, which was looking respectable again.

"I'm going to hang around the one place for a bit." He paused. "Are you coming with us?"

"Let me sleep on it."

I was tempted to join them, until I got back to my room. Still a bit woozy with a headache, I looked in my shoulder bag for a packet of Aspro. A small package fell out. I tore open the wrapping paper to find a silk-bound edition of the Bhagavad Gita—Lord Krishna's spiritual pep talk to warrior-god Arjuna, when he wants to withdraw from battle.

The book opened at a page marked with a red thread. One line stood out: "The seeker knows the joy of Eternity."

I don't know where the book came from, but it told me the journey was still unfinished.

The next day I farewelled my friends at the Perth railway station. We checked out the dining car on the long train and played around with the bunks and fold-away fittings in the sleeper. The station PA announced the departure. Laszlo clasped my shoulder and walked me to the door.

"I hope you find it."

"Keep blowing and don't drink too much," was Thorry's parting advice.

"And you keep practising that drum-roll."

I waited on the platform until the Indian-Pacific pulled out of sight, then caught a cab back to the boat. Nat was standing on the gangway and welcomed me aboard.

"You're in the end cabin. Next stop Bombay."

THE DESTROYER

The first days sailing up the west coast were uneventful. I had time to sit on the deck and write letters in the balmy air of the Indian Ocean. I'd been sending Gary regular journals throughout the trip and owed him an account of the latest events. I also sent Theo a postcard of the Swan River by moonlight, just to show we'd made it. The *Ogun* was scheduled to stop at an oil-rig off Exmouth, where a chopper would carry our mail to the mainland. The ship's company was a mixed lot of Texans, ex-merchant navy, computer technicians and drifters. Nat was a veteran oilman who regaled us with tales of falcon hunting with sheikhs, narrow escapes from border guards and lavish spending in rough dives around the world. He was especially proud of his younger days as a rodeo rough rider, where his ability to ride wild bulls earned him the nickname of The Destroyer.

My cabin mates were less entertaining. The mis-named Angel was a hyper deckhand from Mexico who constantly demanded attention and pestered people to play cards. Bill, an overweight diesel mechanic, was a walking flatulence zone who regularly stank out the small cabin. They bickered constantly and one night Bill had to be stopped from throwing Angel overboard. Apart from *The Horror! The Horror!* this was not Joseph Conrad territory.

The first shoot started off Northwest Cape. The deckhands maintained the hydrophone streamer, logged the survey graphs and tended the guns. During a shoot, explosions assaulted the ocean every fifteen seconds. *Awake Mother, we want your holy fluid.* The data would be used for test drilling in areas where the geological profile showed possible petroleum deposits. At the end of the run, we set course for Sumatra.

The survey routine ended the day we sailed a quiet strait between two small islands. Like hundreds of others in the area, they were apparently uninhabited. I was off-duty, sitting on the stern and blowing sea shanties while watching dolphins play in the wake. After three weeks at sea, I could understand how wishful thinking had created mermaid legends. Nat was leaning, leg raised on a nearby rail, looking at the modern version in a Playboy magazine.

Three fishing-boats approached us from a hidden cove on the port side. The fishermen waved and made friendly gestures, signalling they wanted to come aboard.

"What do you think they want, Nat?"

He gazed intently for a while, then stiffened.

"No nets! And look at the size of those outboards. No ordinary fisherman I've seen around here would have those."

He raced to the bridge, yelled at the captain to hit full speed ahead and re-joined me.

The friendly gestures stopped as we pulled away. A black-prowed boat led the others in pursuit. A short man lifted an AK47 and raked the *Ogun* with a burst of automatic fire. Nat and I dropped for cover behind the bulwark. Some of our crew mates clambered up the companionway behind us to see what was going on. Nat waved them back and another round of bullets pock-marked the hull. Pure fear coursed through my veins. I kept low and still.

"Not exactly the wild beasts you thought you'd tame, eh Orpheus?"

He peered warily above the bulwark.

"I can get that murderous dwarf."

Nat crawled along the deck, down an open hatchway and returned in a minute holding a special-issue Buffalo Bill Winchester with a telescopic sight. Black-prow approached closer. The short man exchanged his AK47 for a rocket-launcher and shouldered it.

Nat raised his deadly third eye and aimed carefully. A drop of sweat appeared on his forehead. A gold ring shaped like a serpent was coiled around his trigger finger. It moved slowly, then jumped with the kick of the rifle, as if striking. The pirate jerked backwards and fell overboard. Nat smiled with grim satisfaction.

"If we make it to the open sea, we're big enough to outrun them through the swell. Otherwise, we're in trouble."

The *Ogun* reached full speed near the end of the strait. The boats closed in, grappling hooks ready. The trawler hit the turbulent waters not far ahead of the pirates. It crashed through the big waves that tossed the smaller vessels around. They lost speed and we watched them dwindle in the distance behind us.

"Those sons-of-bitches are usually happy just to rob and slaughter refugees," said Nat. "Someone's been selling 'em Veetnam hardware, so they're going after bigger fish."

He caught my look of horror and, admittedly, fascination. Nat grabbed my wrist and felt the pulse.

"Not too bad. Perhaps next time you'll be the one behind the rifle."

The sky darkened.

Everyone was shaken by the attack except Nat. He packed his rifle and scope as if they were clubs in a golf-bag.

"Nat, can we sit down for a minute? I've just watched a man shot. Someone who tried to kill us."

"Sorry, minstrel, we ain't gonna sing that song right now. The captain's picked up a cyclone alert and changed course to miss it. We gotta' tie down the equipment and wind in the streamer, so it can't foul the prop."

So that's how you roll, Nat. Action not reflection.

The *Ogun* hit the edge of the cyclone. Large waves lashed the hull. Then the worst happened. The engine stopped, along with the electric power. Bill scrambled down to see what was wrong. He returned, face blackened, holding part of a fuel pump.

"The feed-lines copped some bullets. Water's got into the tank," he shouted above the wind. "It'll take me half-an-hour to fix the pump and connect to a barrel of clean diesel."

Nat set up two teams to drag the oil-filled cable onto the deck and wrap it round the winch. We pulled until exhausted, alternating teams. Warnings were shouted down the line if any bluebottles or other stingers were attached to the cable.

Heavy seas tossed the hapless vessel around. We struggled to keep our balance. Halfway through the haul, the sound of clanging steel containers played an ominous overture.

"Jesus H. Christ, the gas bottles," cursed Nat. "Come on! Let's see if you can dance as well as play."

We staggered over to a storage rack amidships where a dozen cylinders, dislodged by the motion, rolled around the pitching deck.

"Grab 'em by the valve end! If that snaps off, they go like torpedoes and the whole lot could blow up."

He was right about the dancing. We had to grab each 150-pound bottle, lift it back into the rack and tie it down, while avoiding the loose ones that rolled towards us.

"Watch your heel!" yelled Nat as a cylinder raced to crush my foot from behind.

A nifty jeté avoided the rolling brute.

"Trust me. It's character building," said Nat, grinning. "Take a deep breath and dig the adrenaline rush."

We worked furiously in the wet semi-darkness. Despite the cold, we were sweating by the time the last bottle was secured. The welcome hum of the engine started again. The *Ogun* turned and escaped the storm. Nat and I hugged each other with relief.

"May I have this dance?" he said. We waltzed around the deck to whistles and catcalls from the rest of the crew.

"Nat, you sure know how to give someone a good time."

With Bill's constant attention, the *Ogun* managed to reach an ocean oil rig for repairs. Dismissing all protests, Nat pumped the contaminated diesel out of the ship's tank into the ocean. The spreading slick discoloured the water. He probably saw it as some kind of revenge against the elements for giving him a hard time. Bill farted in sympathy and patched up the bullet holes. We refuelled and resumed course for India.

Shipboard life soon settled down to routine again. Bill and Angel resumed their bickering. I looked forward to reaching land.

We reached Bombay Harbour at dusk. The arches and turrets of the Gateway of India appeared in the murky air. Thousands of people milled around the monument to colonial conquest. My first taste of what was in store.

The *Ogun* was scheduled to spend a few days in Bombay to pick up supplies and a relief crew for another regional survey. The deckhands were owed leave and most headed for Goa's beaches. Nat encouraged me to travel overland instead and fly back from Calcutta.

"I envy you seeing India for the first time," he said as I picked up my duffel bag. "Look past the beggars and the sanitation." Nat walked down the gangway with me to the dock.

"Visit Varanasi, if you get the chance."

"What will I find there?"

"The answer to your questions in the little talk we never had."

"Will anything happen about that?"

"Not likely. If it's even reported, it'll be recorded as just another boating accident. Piracy's an established industry there since commercial overfishing deprived the locals of their livelihood.

We shook hands and Nat returned to the boat.

I'll never forget my first day in Bombay. The colour, crowds and chaos. Gaunt children begged in the forecourts of beautiful temples. Women in gold saris walked past people living amongst mounds of rubbish. A naked sadhu wheeled his bicycle over the red carpet in front of a five-star hotel.

The visual impact was overwhelming. A family of 'pinheads' was on show. They performed tricks and squealed at each other, while their 'mother' collected alms. Nearby, street dentists, ear cleaners, tailors and snake charmers impassively plied their trades. A small crowd gathered around a man with his head buried in a hole. Just another day in the office.

Like all first-time visitors I struggled with the meaning of it all. Was I seeing acceptance or indifference? At home, people committed suicide in affluence beyond the dreams of those around me. What life force kept them going?

One day in India and already a philosopher!

A tug on the trouser leg brought me back to earth. I looked down and started. A man with deformed arms and legs was lying on his back. He was painted green with bright red lips. A tin cup was tied on the chest of his distorted torso. I thought of Gary lying far away in the hospital bed and dropped money into the cup. The grotesque figure wriggled away on his back like a worm. The donation attracted other pleading beggars who followed me down the street, pulling at my clothes.

I sought sanctuary in the closest tea-shop. A waiter was wiping dishes, the tables and his face with the same cloth. He scribbled down my order cheerily.

"Yes, sahib, would that be black tea or white tea?"

"White tea, please."

"I'm sorry sahib, we have no milk."

"Black tea, then."

"Certainly, sahib."

I tried to follow the surreal logic of the exchange before storing it in the Funny Travel Stories folder. The waiter was one of Life's gamblers. He knew there was no milk, but offered a false option with a 50/50 chance it would not disappoint.

While waiting for black tea, I read the Bombay Times. The front page headlined complaints by residents of new high rises on Malabar Hill, near the Towers of Silence. The site hosted Parsi funerals where corpses were left outside to be devoured by vultures. The flying undertakers occasionally dropped body parts on the terraces of the upmarket apartments, to the occupants' chagrin. One prominent official was upset his tiffin had been disrupted by "the unwelcome contribution of a rigor-mortised finger to a plate of scones."

An elderly Sikh with a grey beard and a white turban sauntered into the tea-shop and sat at my table. He ordered tea and scones. They arrived on a tray with a small jug of hot milk. So much for my theory. Or perhaps the milk had just been delivered.

"From where are you coming?" asked Major Ranjit Singh (retired) before questioning me about my occupation, salary, marital status and destination. He then listed the places I had to visit, explained the intricacies of Indian rail travel and recommended his brother's guesthouse in Khajuraho.

"You must see the fine erotic sculptures. It's not far out of your way if you're going to Varanasi."

The Major assured me he was also a renowned fortune-teller and offered to read my palm as proof. For twenty rupees. We settled on ten if I picked up the bill. He squinted at my hand through thick, black-rimmed glasses and consulted a battered notebook.

"I see you are a wanderer on a quest," he pronounced with an air of revelation. "Your lifeline is crossed in three places. You are approaching the second junction and will soon have to make a decision that will change your destiny."

"What will happen?"

"The heartline shows the decision should be made by the heart, not the head. The third crossing is deeper and more serious, but some time away. You have special gifts, but there is still much young man's nonsense to be dealt with."

He brushed away my questions and peered closer.

"A stranger will trust you with a mission. If you accept and betray him, there will be serious consequences. You will also face betrayal. Fear death by water." (And T.S. Eliot?)

"Thank you for such eclectic insight, Major. Did you ever run a music school?"

He closed the book, finished the tea and presented his own hand. For the ten rupees.

"I must be going. Should you visit Agra, it is by moonlight the Taj Mahal is most beautiful."

I stayed another two days in Bombay, then set off to Delhi. The trains were hot, noisy and crowded. People rode perilously on the roof, ducking the tunnels. Steam engines lost their romance when the gritty black smoke blew in the window. The toilets were surreal and I had to keep reminding myself not to get hung up on it. But my fellow passengers were outgoing and friendly, with long lists of questions about life in Australia.

We passed palaces, mud huts, lush farmlands and dry plots where farmers eked out a grim medieval existence. Railway crossings were living museums with lines of Morris sedans and Royal Enfield motorbikes from the 1950s. I was told that a legendary 350 cc model was worshipped at the Bullet Baba Temple outside Jodhpur. Apparently, the bike kept returning at night to the accident site where its owner was killed

Delhi station was a spectacle of millions of people on the move. Families camped and cooked on platforms, while chai wallahs, fruit vendors, porters, pilgrims, mystics and salesmen of all kinds paraded up and down yelling, chanting or singing.

I explored the city for a day. For some reason, Connaught Circus and the radial streets made me think of Canberra. The gates, narrow alleys and bazaars of old Delhi were fascinating, but I was more interested in reaching Agra. The easy morning run on the Taj Express was long enough for all fellow passengers in the compartment to get to know each other.

The erudite and amiable Mr. Kumar commandeered attention.

"We are crossing the Yamuni River and the Taj Mahal stands right beside it. Did you know that an echo will resonate there for eighteen seconds?" He adjusted his dhoti and pointed out the window.

"Further upstream is where Krishna sported with the gopis, and stole their clothes while they were bathing. They were taking refreshment from tending their cows."

My self-appointed guide warmed to his subject.

"The story is that Krishna physically multiplied himself so he could make love to all of the gopis. A most useful attribute, I think you would agree."

The male passengers nodded in agreement, as we pulled into the station.

"Goodbye, Mr. Chris. A truly blessed name, I think. Chris, Christ, Krishna. Chryses was one of Apollo's priests, I recall."

I thanked him for his commentary and we exchanged addresses. He had cast a whole new light on my visit to Agra and planted an idea. The hotel he recommended was a short walk from the station. Like some ancient mariner, I passed a wedding group on the way and stopped one of the guests to ask directions.

I checked in, dumped my bag on the bed and looked out the window. The clouds were parting. A perfect night to follow the Major's advice.

The Taj Mahal shimmered serenely under the full moon. A frozen symphony in white, its tall minarets reaching longingly upwards. I wandered around the gardens to admire the curved, feminine dome from all angles. I walked into the huge central chamber. Mr. Kumar was right. It had a superb echo. However, too many people were crowded there for my purposes.

I hid in the gardens just before midnight and waited for the gates to close. I crept back inside and stopped at the tombs of Emperor Shah Jahan and Mumtaz Mahal, the tragic love of his life. The light filtered through the carved screens and played across the inlaid patterns of semi-precious stones.

I pulled out my harp and addressed the tombs. "Well, guys, you had a Frenchman help decorate this place so you might like a little Debussy. How about Pierrot's love song?"

The sounds of Claire de Lune soared to the top of the chamber and resounded like a thousand-voice choir. With a power of its own, the music drifted out across the gardens, through the red gateway to the river. It flowed past the grove to where Krishna sat on a bed of scented leaves with Radha, his favourite gopi. He picked up his flute and accompanied the melody. Its pain, joy, passion and discipline summed up the lessons of the Road. I realised all four are needed to play—and to live—fully.

The Taj watchman had the grace to wait until I finished playing before throwing me out.

"Quite a conceit," he said. "A venue dedicated to love, an epiphany and a French Impressionist gig with the gods of India."

Now that's a cool watchman!

Technically, the Major was correct. Khajuraho was not far out of the way. But it was a slow, bumpy bus ride from Agra the following day.

"I hope it's worth being rolled and tossed like a chapati for twelve hours to see a stone version of the Kama Sutra," I thought after the third breakdown. "Am I destined to travel on mechanical disasters the rest of my life? Patience, patience. India takes patience."

Khajuraho was a hot, dry and dusty village. The Major's brother greeted me as if we were old friends. He was an identical twin of the original and a retired Major as well.

"Yes, it was most confusing during our army service," he admitted, waggling his head. "But my brother's a bigger scoundrel and I don't tell fortunes."

The guesthouse was a small, clean bungalow not far from the temples. The Major suggested I visit them in the cool of the early morning.

The sandstone shrines were set on terraces in a quiet rural setting. They were adorned with exquisite carvings of another world, with gods, goddesses, warriors, musicians, beautiful dancing women, animals and mythical beasts.

As I stared at the thousand-year-old carvings on one temple, the images of sexual delight came alive. I watched the full-breasted apsaras and their lovers shamelessly enjoying all possible (and impossible) positions and combinations. This time, the life force was joy.

The carvings also celebrated everyday activities with women shown washing their hair, applying makeup or carrying flowers. Others luxuriated in poses reminiscent of Nat's centrefolds. One looked out straight at me. I could swear it was Rati.

Perhaps I'd been too single-minded that night in the hills about going on the road. Or maybe I'd just been travelling alone for too long.

Over afternoon tea on the veranda, the Major said no one could explain why the temples were built in such an out-of-the way place, but there may have been a religious reason.

"Religious?" I asked sceptically, thinking about the erotic images.

"It might be hard for someone from the West to understand," he reprimanded. "But many in India believe the act of union combines man and woman bodily and spiritually so that each becomes both. The energy lovers feel flowing through their bodies is seen as a form of the divine energy that generates and sustains the world."

"I'm sorry if I offended you, Major. You've reminded me that my views on religion may be too narrow."

He waved away the apology and changed the subject.

"My boy picked up your tickets to Varanasi, while you were out. You're on the evening bus. Make an effort to see the ghats at dawn, when you arrive."

"Thank you, Major. I will. The advice from both of you has been very sound."

The bus was half empty and the Major had reserved the whole back seat for me. I was able to stretch out and sleep, disturbed only by the odd erotic vision of a threesome that defied gravity.

I awoke to morning light in the city of Shiva and headed straight for the Ganges when I got off the bus. Men of all ages greeted the sun with yoga exercises on the steps by the river. Thousands of pilgrims bathed in the holy water and made offerings. Priests blessed the faithful. A body floated by, chomped by carnivorous turtles.

I passed monkeys scampering around Durga Temple and came upon a funeral procession. A white-swathed body was carried to one of the burning ghats. It joined the never-ending succession of cremations. The mourners gathered around the fire, oblivious to the passers-by. The smell of burning flesh mingled with the scent of sandalwood as the keeper of the flames stoked the fire with a large stick.

For the first time in my life, I watched my own mortality.

The shroud and the flesh were quickly consumed. A burning arm raised and pointed upwards as if still alive. The skull exploded. I jumped at the sound. Pieces of bone flew out of the fire and showered the onlookers. The keeper smashed the ribcage, to ensure it burnt properly. A hawker walked through the group to sell me postcards. No one grieved openly. I'd been to more serious barbeques.

I spent hours wandering around the ghats and temples. Near Gyan Kupor, the "Well of Knowledge," I heard Varanasi's soundtrack. A man with an ash-covered face squatted in front of a harmonium. He fingered the keyboard with his right hand and pumped the blue bellows with his left. The temporal rhythms and spiritual melodies played against each other and then resolved themselves into one, just as Varanasi had. The music resounded within me for days and stayed there.

The break was nearly over. Was it only three weeks? I treated myself to a first-class sleeper for the final leg of the journey. I thought I'd seen it all, but Calcutta seemed to have even more crowds and slums than anywhere else along the way. According to Nat, the city also had more flower-sellers and poetry magazines.

First stop was the Great Oriental Hotel to check the oil company's agent for messages and forwarded mail. I passed a narrow back street where a small group gathered around a broken pipe jutting out of a mildewed wall. They joked and laughed amongst themselves as they washed in this city oasis or drank from rusty old tins.

A man with a goitre the size of a small football passed a drink to a half-man, missing from almost the waist down. He rested on a piece of scrap wood attached to some old furniture-wheels. An older man, with a back broken into a W shape, leant on a stick at right-angles and chatted to his noseless, limbless and blind colleagues.

Welcome to Club Calcutta, meeting place for the Children of God.

I watched unseen, at first, and felt ashamed. Ashamed of a world that could accept such conditions. And envious of the joy I had seen. A joy that had emerged through pain. But was it despite the pain, or was pain necessary to achieve joy, as the saints had argued?

The inner musings ended as soon as the group spotted me. Angry stares and muttered curses were aimed at the rich, white traveller sailing over the world's woes in a glass-bottomed boat. How could I restore what I had taken?

Not quite heavenly, but perhaps the harp could help. A slow, bluesy version of an old folk hymn came out. Surprised at first, the group went silent and listened. A wailing voice from somewhere joined the second chorus.

I'm just a poor wayfaring stranger
Travelling through this world of woe
There is no sickness, no toil, nor danger
In that bright land to which I go

"Thank you, Traveller," said W. "I enjoyed the melody, but I believe the words are misleading."

"Not so," said Man on Wheels. "We must believe them, or there's no hope."

Others disagreed and an ontological debate broke out.

I moved on.

The Great Oriental was a block away. An era away. Potted palms, lace tablecloths and waiters wearing white jackets surmounted by turbans with peacock feathers. I picked up my mail and eagerly went through the bundle of envelopes in the faded glory of the Raj Tea-Room. A telegram offered a new contract with Golden Petroleum and a reminder the ship was leaving Bombay at the end of the week.

There was also a letter from Sibyl. It started with friendly greetings and some gossip. The tone changed with a request not to let Gary know she'd written.

> I'm sorry I misled you and the others about
> the golden prospects in the West. I admit I
> was trying to get rid of you for selfish rea-
> sons. I was jealous of Gary's loyalties to you
> and the group and felt I could not compete.
> I also blamed you all for the accident. I
> realise now I share that blame by trying to
> stop him going to the buck's night.

Gary is coping badly. He would have full mobility in his arms and hands if he did his exercises. But he's going down and has lost the will to do anything. I caught him saving up his sleeping pills. Our son, Jason, has been born. He is beautiful but Gary says a cripple is useless as a father. Perhaps I'm being selfish again in asking this, but I believe you and the music might save him. Could you find it in your heart to return?

DIE AT THE RIGHT TIME

The letter drooped in my hand. I placed it on the white tablecloth and poured hot milk into my tea from the sterling silver jug. I felt pulled in two directions. Another challenge from Sibyl and another crossroad. The choice was clear. I could board the flight to Bombay the next morning and sail off. A life of travel, adventure... and a regular salary. Not so much music perhaps, but living on the edge with people like Nat. The alternative was to heed the call of friendship and return home to an uncertain future, without knowing whether or not I could really help Gary.

Before India, the decision might have been different. But the brief journey had showed made me life's transience and the importance of hope. Recalling the Major's words in Bombay, I hoped his readings were more accurate than his itineraries. I counted my traveller's cheques, flicked through the Lonely Planet guide and made some quick calculations. I had enough time and money to reach Kuala Lumpur for a cheap flight back to Melbourne.

I spotted a pile of hotel postcards on a nearby hall-stand. The old photograph showed the building in the flush of proud Victorian optimism, before decay set in. I tore up three cards trying to get the message right. I wanted to sound casual and pretend not to know what was really happening with Gary, while giving him a prod.

> I've left the ship. My heart wasn't in it. I should be home by the time you leave hospital. I've collected some great new sounds and want to get the group back together. So, dust off your axe and check out some Eastern scales.
>
> Hi to Sibyl. Okay if I bunk at your place the first couple of nights?

I posted the card at the reception desk where I sent a brief telegram to Nat saying I had to return home. Letter to follow.

As I walked out into the crowded streets again, I realised life had become a journey on the two paths of my hallucination in the chain locker. The known and the unknown. The real and the fantastic. Great insight, but I was still returning home broke and far from the celestial highway fantasy.

A packed tram passed with people hanging all over it. Iron spikes on the front discouraged passengers from blocking the driver's window. The seer must be protected.

I followed the map to Sudder Street and spent my last night in India at the Salvation Army Hostel, a popular centre for travellers and information. Students going the other way said Burma's land borders were closed, so it meant flying to Bangkok. From there, it was an easy run hitching to Kuala Lumpur or using local transport.

Next morning's mini-bus ride to Dum-Dum Airport offered a final paradox. Towering over a huge area of shanty slums, a large billboard advertised a gleaming new car and proclaimed that *Going Ford is the Going Thing*.

The airport departure lounge was the gateway to another world. The neutral decor made it hard to believe I was in India, or had even spent time there. The Bangkok flight was late and waiting passengers complained aloud when a three-hour delay was announced. Life's problems had assumed a different scale.

Looking around for diversion, I noticed a blond Nordic couple. He performed magic tricks for two restless children sitting nearby, while she leant on a guitar case and cheered him on. A lively performer in a bright, batik shirt, his hair was cropped unusually short for the time. She was more composed and pretended to ignore the stares at her revealing hot pants. The attractive pair clearly enjoyed being the centre of attention. She caught my eye and smiled. After exhausting a repertoire of handkerchief and coin tricks, he went to the bar and returned with drinks and candies.

Time dragged by. The woman unpacked the guitar—the latest high-tech Ovation, made of black carbon fibre. I thought it could have sounded better for the price, but she strummed some chords that turned into an impressive version of a Luiz Bonfá Brazilian classic. Her lack of self-consciousness was catching. I walked over, harp in hand.

"Mind if I join you? I just happen to know Samba de Orfeu."

We clicked as if we'd been performing together for years. She sang with a strong, sultry voice, while I weaved around the melody. I then took a chorus with her accompaniment. An audience of other passengers gathered around us and clapped at the end, asking for more. A drink found my hand.

"Too easy," she said and broke into an eerie version of the popular Canto de Ossanha—a warning against the use of love spells in Candomblé ceremonies.

"Do you really believe love is only good if it hurts?" I asked.

"How else do you know if you're alive?"

The impromptu concert created a festive mood that kept us playing until the flight arrival was announced. Some of the passengers thanked us for the performance before lining up at the boarding gate. One of them was a dapper, middle-aged man wearing an Italian suit and a gold Rolex. Raja Harimau passed us his card.

"I enjoyed your music very much. Are you heading towards Malaysia?"

"It's possible," said the woman.

He smiled and bowed slightly.

"If you reach Kuala Lumpur in about ten days, please call me. I would like to have you perform at my wife's birthday party. She adored Brazil."

First-class boarding was announced. He excused himself and walked to the gate.

"You two do sound good together," said the conjuror offering his hand. "My name's John Locke. No relation, but my father was English and not very liberal," he added, to avoid the usual question. "My friends call me Loki. And this is Freya. Yes, yes. The Trickster and the Sea Goddess. Two gods at once. Just a coincidence."

We shook hands and exchanged compliments.

"The flight's not full. Let's see if we can get our seats swapped round to sit together," Freya suggested. "I see I have a kindred musical spirit."

Loki was an outgoing charmer and a continual joker. He ordered drinks and teased the flight attendant by using sleight-of-hand to make the glasses disappear.

Despite the flow of conversation, they were both evasive about where they'd been or where they were going.

She performed *all over*, but it was a *sideline*. He patted his short hair and said his head looked like an albino toilet-brush because of a stint in a Buddhist monastery near the Chinese border.

"There's fighting up there?"

"Something like that. Didn't affect me. Too busy seeking enlightenment. I'm now working with an aid project for the Montagnards."

"From the French Revolution?"

"Non, non, it means *highlander*. It's what they call Hmong people from the central highlands of Vietnam."

"Why them?"

He became serious for once. "They're a persecuted minority fighting the North. I help get medical supplies to their base in eastern Cambodia."

"Why isn't America doing that?"

"Uncle Sam's screwing them. He still hasn't realised that betrayal is like poisoning a well you will drink from one day."

The seat-belt lights came on and Freya lightened the conversation by asking me where I was staying in Bangkok. I shrugged.

"You might find the Nirvana Hotel interesting. We can share the taxi."

After we landed, the cab ride to the hotel took three hours, dodging kamikaze tuk-tuks through the clogged, polluted streets. During one prolonged stop, the driver handed us a printed plastic menu in three languages. It showed an order-by-number list of activities offered by the "City of Angels."

He rattled off the most popular pursuits, then moved onto the more select offerings when there were no takers.

"Young boy? Young girl? Orgy? Ping pong show? Lady with dog?" Then in a lowered voice: "Snuff movie?"

I handed back the menu.

"Haven't you got anything kinky?"

The driver looked puzzled and checked both sides.

"The movie offer is new one, since we were here last," said Freya.

"I love to see the dynamism of the free market in action," added Loki.

The disappointed driver tossed the menu aside. "Maybe you like temple tour instead?"

The Nirvana Hotel was a nondescript medium-rise thrown together on the edge of town for R&R soldiers and backpackers. Staff treated guests as intrusions and demanded cash up front for food, services or phone calls. The lobby needed a paint job and new carpets, but management had more important concerns than trifles such as maintenance—or passports.

A large notice-board near the creaky elevator hosted dozens of pinned messages. They offered motorbikes, one-way air tickets, *army surplus equipment* and *personal travel companions*. Meetings were set up for *the usual place* and a *professional pest exterminator* provided a post-office box address

Stringy, road-weary travellers with Nepalese shoulder-bags mingled with soldiers, students and the lumpy-jacket-with-aluminium-briefcase brigade. Loki warned that a French serial killer and his girlfriend occasionally dropped by to poison and rob unsuspecting Westerners.

In other words, Nirvana Hotel was irresistible. And after some of India's 'budget' accommodations, the place was Modern Luxury, with a bar, swimming pool and a soundtrack of the latest pirate tapes.

The receptionists were busy talking and ignored us. Loki teased them into action by slapping the counter-bell loudly and making it vanish when he lifted his hand.

One of the women recognised him. "You again? I see they give you nice haircut. No trouble this time, okay?"

"Never trouble," replied Loki innocently and asked for two separate rooms. He pulled out a few passport photos of himself and Freya.

"Got any spare ones?" he asked me. "This will come in useful."

He handed over all the photos to the woman with a hundred-baht note.

"Please tell our friend I want to see him today."

We went to our rooms, cleaned up and changed. Freya wanted to go shopping and I felt like a swim. Loki joined me.

The pool was landscaped with broken deck-chairs and forlorn pot-plants, but the water looked inviting. A sign by the diving-board decreed: *Bar-girls are banned for hygienic reasons.*

"The long-term stayers wanted that," said Loki, reading my thoughts. "A weird VD's getting about that's penicillin-resistant. There's supposed to be an island in the Gulf of Siam where they keep soldiers who've caught it."

"A modern-day leper colony?"

He nodded. "My GI friends claim some of the Americans reported missing in action are really wasting away there. The authorities are afraid to send them back."

"Somehow I don't think swimming pools are the problem."

"No, but a little reminder for a young man who's been on the road solo for some time to keep himself pure."

A little reminder in more ways than one, I thought.

Loki swam with me for a while, then excused himself, saying he had to meet someone.

"Come up for a drink before dinner," he suggested in a tone that assumed I would.

I kept swimming. Travelling with Loki and Freya was like getting on a mystery train. They could be as charming, seductive and full of wiles as their namesakes.

Freya would look at me knowingly one minute and then hug Loki. He would leave us alone sometimes and come back all possessive. Both loved an audience and I often had trouble getting a word in. It was a game they kept inviting me to join and I was carried along by their energy.

That evening, I knocked on their door. Freya was re-stringing her guitar. Loki sat on the floor, cross-legged, smoking a bronze, dragon-shaped pipe.

"Met an old friend, just back from Laos." He offered me the pipe. "Good shit. Keeps the boys going in Vietnam. Blurs the line between right and wrong."

I shook my head. "Thanks anyway. That stuff doesn't agree with me."

Loki feigned disappointment, passed the pipe to Freya and got up.

"Ah, perhaps we can tempt you with something else. Have you tried this?"

He opened a flask of the local whisky.

"Costs all of a dollar and according to the stamp is three weeks old. A vintage for the Mekong label! A bit rough, but not too bad with a liberal splash of Coke."

He passed me the glass and I drank dutifully.

"Here, look what else I got us."

He handed me a forged student pass with my photo on it.

"This'll help you buy tickets for those charter flights. There's a whole load of students coming over for the Thaipusam festival."

He handed me another laminated card.

"International press pass. Very handy for getting into places, especially trouble zones."

I thanked him and slipped the cards into my passport pouch.

"Let's eat," said Freya.

"Ever the practical one, when it comes to the senses."

"You don't do too badly yourself."

They chased each other down the corridor to the elevator. She pressed the Up button.

The doors opened and we stepped inside. A faulty neon flickered on and off with the disorienting effect of a strobe light.

"Amazing things, elevators," said Loki.

A stone rave coming on, I thought.

"They carry you through space at high speed. Up and down. Penthouse to basement. Heaven to hell and back again."

Freya's face lit up with excitement. She'd been through this before.

"You can stop at any level," he continued.

"Each floor a different world, a different experience," she added.

He pointed to the buttons.

"Look, no thirteenth floor. Man has just landed on the moon, but the ancient fears still prevail."

He pressed the twelfth-floor button. What was this leading to?

The doors opened. "One small step for ancient man," declared Loki.

He and Freya leapt out of the lift. They bounded up the corridor laughing and mimicking the clumsy gait of astronauts. Their play was so infectious I found myself joining them. We bounced out the doors at the end of the corridor onto a balcony. A million lights in the streets far below moved like fireflies, each emitting its own aura through the smog.

Loki sprang up suddenly and balanced on the railing, his arms outstretched. I reached forward instinctively to grab him.

"It's all right," said Freya and leapt up to join him. "We will ourselves to rise high."

She swayed, then balanced on one leg, kicking upwards with the other, in a well-practised martial arts movement.

"Is that Capoeira?"

"I joined the Mestre Bimba school in Bahia. The slaves saw it as a way to freedom."

"Learn how to dance beyond yourselves," said Loki.

"I see you've found your niche," I retorted.

Bad pun.

He spun on the railing to face me.

"Don't be such a Philosophy One clever-dick! You hide behind your harp and your music, Orpheus."

"If you want to rise high above the underworld, you must stop looking back," said Freya.

"Join us."

They were tempting me to enter their world. But first I had to pass a test. Why not? I thought. If I can survive pirates, cyclones and Indian buses. I clambered up to the railing carefully and looked down. Terrified and swaying.

"Savour the fear," said Loki. "The adrenaline. The sweat. Turn it into pleasure. Laugh at the abyss." He quoted again: "Learn to die at the right time."

A surge of energy displaced the fear. I walked across the railing towards them, chugging the riff to Midnight Flyer. Loki and Freya applauded. We all jumped back onto the balcony, laughing and embracing.

"I'm even more hungry," said Freya

The dinner was manic. Loki entertained the whole room juggling glasses, bottles and cutlery and making them vanish. Not to be outdone, Freya set a goblet of brandy alight and somehow downed it. I played the circus music.

When we quietened down, Loki reached into his pocket and pulled out a filigree necklace, set with rubies.

"I believe this is yours, daughter of the sea-god," he said formally.

Freya looked at him with disbelief, her eyes moist.

"Tears of gold," he said, brushing them away gently.

Once again, I was an outsider, watching events with an unknown history.

He attached the necklace around her neck. The rubies lit up with an internal flame. Loki kissed her cheek and returned to his chair.

"I have to leave you for a while," he announced. "There was a message summoning me to Cambodia for a few days. I'm going early tomorrow."

The atmosphere turned sombre as Freya's smile faded.

"I must repay a debt for the freedom to be here tonight. I'll meet you in Kuala Lumpur in a week. The usual place."

He turned to me. "I know I can charge you to look after her."

Freya and I exchanged looks as Loki asked for the bill. We returned to our rooms in silence.

Freya and I met next morning at the travel office. All flights to Kuala Lumpur were booked out because of Thaipusam. Going overland was the only way.

"We can take the overnight bus to the border," said Freya. "And then catch one of those old Mercedes cabs they run down to KL."

"You sure know your way around the world."

"I've travelled a lot since I lost my husband," she replied, as if thinking aloud.

"Your...?"

"Let's find the bus station," she interrupted, realising what had slipped out. "We can do that temple tour this afternoon."

The Hanuman Express was a large comfortable coach with reclining seats. A far cry from my last bus trip. I helped Freya with her bags and stored the guitar case in the shelf above us. The other passengers were mainly westerners. A smiling hostess handed out paper cups of Coke.

"They're still doing it," said Freya. "Pour it out on the carpet when no one's looking and hand her back the empty cup."

The coach glided quietly out of the terminal and the driver switched off the interior lights. By the time we reached the main southern highway, the other passengers were slumped in a heavy sleep.

"Just watch."

The bus stopped by the side of the road and the door opened. A young Thai couple entered quietly and started rifling through the accessible packs and shoulder bags. I rose out of my seat as they approached, but Freya dragged me back. The man pulled a knife out of his jeans and flicked the blade open. The woman grabbed his arm. He shrugged, cursed under his breath and followed her outside again. The driver pretended not to see anything. The door closed and the bus started on its way.

"You males love confrontation," said Freya. "Sometimes it's better to observe than participate. The police are part of this one, so there's no point in making a fuss."

We reached the border at dawn, when some of the passengers began to stir.

"Most comfortable trip I've had in ages," said a man behind us. "I can't believe how well I slept."

Exit stamps at the Thai border were a brief formality. But at the Malaysian post, two armed men in uniform ordered all passengers to line up with their luggage.

Freya struggled with her bags, so once again I helped with the guitar case. Before I could pass it back to her, I was shepherded into the customs area. A sign behind the counter warned of the death penalty for anyone caught smuggling *dadah* into Malaysia.

Behind the counter, a short, stocky man in uniform went through my pack expertly. He squeezed the toothpaste tube, felt the clothes and opened my guide book. I started feeling very uneasy about the guitar case and how little I knew about Freya and her travels.

Savour the fear. Turn it into pleasure.

The adrenaline felt good. It sharpened the senses. I could smell the magnolias outside the customs shed. Two frogs in a nearby pond croaked what sounded like the intro to a Canned Heat number. I relaxed into a smile just as the customs man pulled my harp out of its case.

He looked at the engraved symbol with delight.

"Iban sign," he said. "From my area. Very strong. Gives protection."

He pressed the chromatic button quizzically and handed me the harp. I demonstrated with the opening bars of Bullfrog Blues.

"If you are a musician, you will find Sarawak very interesting," he said, making friendly small talk as he opened the guitar case. Its presence no longer bothered me.

"You're a long way from home, then."

"My village is gone," he replied. "We were moved when they cut the forest to sell the wood and plant palm-oil trees."

"I'm sorry to hear that."

"I was lucky. I have a job," he replied, unconvinced.

He lifted the guitar out, looked inside it and poked the case padding. Satisfied, he helped me pack up and wished me well. Freya was waiting outside.

"Sounds like you had a concert in there."

I looked into her calm, blue eyes. No sign of any concern or relief. Either very innocent or very good.

"You didn't have anything to worry about?" she said ambiguously.

"It seems not."

An old Mercedes teksi was waiting outside the customs office. We agreed on the fare to KL and settled into the worn seats. The rattling, diesel cab stopped often to pick up or drop off other passengers, so the journey took all day.

The Indian driver, Varghese, enjoyed pointing out the sights and talked about his family scattered along the whole route. He took us to his cousin's curry stall, his uncle's cake shop and finally his sister's homestay in Kuala Lumpur.

"You must go to Thaipusam. Very interesting. It's now banned in India, so people come from all around the world to see it here. You won't believe your eyes."

When the cab was full, Freya and I were pressed up against each other in the back seat. Her warmth and sweat mingled with mine. She slept with her head on my shoulder part of the way and I felt her strong, lean body through the thin cotton clothing. A tension was growing between us. She defused it by talking about Loki, although their backgrounds and plans remained a mystery. All she revealed was that they had some business in Indonesia after he re-joined her in KL.

That night, at least, there was no occasion to pursue the matter. The long, hot trip had tired us out. Varghese dropped us off at his sister's house. Freya asked for two separate rooms before the question came up.

The next day she took me to a travel office that accepted my student pass for a charter flight ticket to Melbourne. We walked back through the city. KL was a mixture of high-rise blocks, colonial buildings, a Chinatown and an ornate Moorish railway station. Freya pointed to a mansion in the middle of town.

"That's where I'm meeting Loki on Friday night. There's not much else that interests me here, but I'd like to see Thaipusam."

We found a bus to the Batu Caves. The approach to the festival site was packed with buses, cars, tents, stalls and huge crowds. Police cleared a path for the thousands of Lord Subramaniam's devotees who staggered in a trance up the steps of the limestone caverns. Many had spikes in their tongues or long, steel spears through both cheeks. Others carried offerings of fruit dangling from hooks that pierced their backs and chests. Some bore heavy, decorated frames with religious displays, supported by long sharp spikes piercing their torsos.

A punk picnic gone berserk.

Freya and I watched fascinated. Not a drop of blood or sign of pain anywhere. Painted men cracked bullwhips to keep the surging crowd away from the procession as it made its way to a shrine inside the main cave. The hot, hypnotic atmosphere was thick with incense and the chanting of prayers, punctuated by a drum beat and the sound of smashing coconuts. I almost felt like joining in.

Priests removed the hooks and spikes, rubbing grey ash into the body areas where the holes should have been. No marks were left on the devotees as they emerged from their trance. We watched the ceremony until dawn, then returned to town.

"Loki would love this," said Freya. "It's about will overcoming the impossible."

At the mention of his name, she became quiet and sat apart from me, lost in her thoughts.

We still had four days before my flight to Melbourne and Freya's reunion with Loki. Was I going to spend the entire time visiting mosques and museums?

We arrived at the guesthouse and a business card fell out of my wallet as I paid the fare.

"Why don't we ring that Raja Harimau we met at Calcutta airport?" I said, breaking the silence.

"Why not?"

I called the number from a phone in the hallway. A woman answered.

"Raja has left the office and gone back to his home in Kuching. There are MAS airline tickets waiting for you at the domestic airport. He would be honoured if you could play at his wife's birthday and be his guest for a few days."

I hung up the phone.

"Freya, how do you feel about a gig in Borneo? We'd be back by Friday."

"Could be interesting," she said walking to her room. "See you tonight."

The veranda was cool that evening. I sat in a rattan chair, playing a slow blues.

In the moonlit courtyard, Freya pirouetted, cartwheeled and pounced through a capoeira routine. Was Loki the shadow by her side, moving in harmony, or was he the invisible opponent? She finished with a leap and a powerful kick that made the sound of rushing wind above her head.

She walked past me on the way back to her room and paused.

"Goodnight."

"Goodnight."

The flight from the mainland to Sarawak took less than two hours. I picked up a Malay Post in the seat pocket. Savage clashes south of Kuching, along the Indonesian border, led the front page. Dayak warriors armed with spears and machetes had beheaded thirty loggers and eaten them. *Miscreants, murders and meals* said the headline.

The report described heads, hearts and livers brandished on the points of spears. You gotta' love tabloids. I left my beef satay and looked out the window.

The descent to Kuching airport took us over dense tracts of jungle. Large deforested areas stood out like leprous sores. Barges floated down the river, loaded with logs for disposable chopsticks, takeaway coffee stirrers and office paper. Rainforest Liberation had been right.

A driver and a gold Mercedes were waiting for us outside the terminal and took us to Raja Harimau's house. On a hill overlooking the Sarawak River, Mount Ophir resembled a small Taj Mahal. A moat surrounded the marble mansion. A waterfall flowed into a pool that extended under the house wall into the living room.

Raja's wife, Kumang, greeted us warmly at the door. A beautiful younger woman wearing Chanel, with a diamond and yellow gold necklace to match. Raja sat on a white whale-skin couch playing a Villa Lobos prelude on a handmade guitar of rare timbers.

He put it down when he saw us and rose to shake hands.

"Nice piece you were playing," I said.

He nodded deferentially in Freya's direction.

"Just an amateur, I'm afraid. I took it up at Oxford. No time to practise, but it relaxes me."

He ordered tea and we made polite conversation about our travels.

"My husband told me about the Brazilian numbers you perform," said Kumang. "I fell in love with the music when we were there last year."

"Was it a holiday?" asked Freya.

"Not for me," said Raja. "I was looking at their rainforest harvesting in Amazonia. I try to keep up with the latest methods."

116

I'd never heard rape called harvesting before, but we were guests.

"On the plane I read about some trouble over that issue south of here."

His face became serious.

"My wife's people can't go running round the jungle for ever. We're trying to give them proper housing, schools. Civilisation."

"Our guests must be tired," interrupted Kumang. "Come, I'll show you to your rooms. You may care to rest after the flight. Perhaps you need some laundry done for tonight. We can discuss the program a little later on."

"That's a beautiful guitar," said Freya. "It sounds much better than mine. May I borrow it for the party?"

"By all means," said Raja. "I'll be interested to see what you can do with it."

I was led to a luxurious room, where I soaked in the spa, musing over the ups and downs of the Road. From bedbugs and terror to luxury and fascination. A target one day, a king the next. I'd been stretched in all directions lately—except one.

I dressed and went downstairs to the ballroom, where I could hear Freya playing.

"I've worked out a program with Kumang. They're all numbers we know, but we'd better rehearse a bit."

The party was a discreet, elegant affair. The thirty select guests included politicians, film stars, millionaires and embassy people. Raja had lent me a formal batik shirt in blue and white. Freya looked like a fairy-tale princess magnificent in a light-blue designer outfit she'd borrowed from Kumang.

The performance went down very well. Freya's songs of love and yearning carried the audience to Ipanema Beach where the harp and guitar harmonies caressed each other like waves on the Atlantic shore. I wished life would imitate art.

After the performance, Freya and I circulated amongst the guests. Raja was very pleased with the evening and approached me after they left.

"I have to go up-river tonight, on a goodwill mission. It would help if you could join me for a men's gathering at an Iban longhouse. You might find it interesting to see what I've been talking about."

Freya had other plans. She came into my room as I was changing.

"Do you realise this is our last night together? Why don't you spend it with me?"

She kissed me passionately. I held her and returned the kiss. But something felt wrong. Why now? I looked at her face and could see Loki in her eyes.

Betrayal is a poison... I charge you to look after her.

"What about Loki?"

She turned cold, pushed me away and walked to her room.

"Can we talk about this?"

Her door slammed.

Raja was waiting in his sleek Varuna speedboat by the landing below the house. I clambered aboard and his driver started the twin outboards.

We powered up the wide, silent river, past the deforested areas outside Kuching, to where the jungle was thick again. The boat stopped at a small jetty by a village. Three men greeted us with distant formality. We followed them up a track to a wooden longhouse built on stilts. They climbed a notched log to the main doorway.

"Take off your shoes and wait until we're invited," said Raja.

Threatening faces carved into the door greeted us, but the meeting place inside was festive and welcoming. The men were dressed in traditional, woven cottons and beaded jackets. I was directed to a timber platform and handed a glass of potent rice tuak. My companions kindly showed me how to down the glass in one shot—so it could be refilled quickly.

Human skulls mouldered on the rafters. A large gong hung by the entrance, adorned with an ouroboros dragon eating its own tail. A brass, crocodile-shaped cannon stood ready in the corner. The missionaries must have had a busy time.

Raja was asked to join the chief at the other end of the gallery. Their conversation became animated, then heated. A powerful-looking man, wearing a feathered warrior headdress, made threatening gestures with his machete. Raja excused himself and came over.

"I'm in a little trouble here," he said quietly. "They're fired up over what happened on the border. But they're holding back out of respect for their honoured guest."

"Me?"

"I told them you were a famous musician. Please humour our hosts."

"I'm not sure, but I'll see what I can do."

"Makai," announced the chief, signifying that food was coming. Bowls of stew were passed around. He made a comment and everyone laughed.

"What did he say Raja?"

"Meat from the south. Very tender."

"Is he serious or just messing with us?"

"I don't know. But try to eat at least some of it, or you'll offend them."

"Okay, Raja. Stew's stew, I guess."

I closed my eyes, swallowed a mouthful and drank a glass of tuak to keep it down.

I put the bowl on the platform with signs that it was delicious, wondering what I'd eaten. To change the subject, I asked about the blowgun tournament starting across the room—the local version of pub darts. The target was a straw effigy on the far wall. I remembered the game we played with lengths of pipe on the banks of the Kananook. Only the Vegemite was missing, this time.

The competitors were noisy, enthusiastic and very accurate. The darts sped to their mark and clustered around the heart of the straw man. I was invited to join the match and felt challenged to meet the standard.

When my turn came, I took a deep breath and aimed carefully. Just then, a large rat scampered across the rafter above my head. As if by instinct, I swung the blowgun up and fired. Bullseye! The hapless rodent fell to the floor skewered.

"Manah! Manah!" cheered my fellow hunters and pronounced me winner. The prize: another glass.

The atmosphere was loosening up and Raja looked less worried. An old Iban produced a Sape and started plucking the large paddle-shaped instrument. One string was tuned as a constant drone for the Arabic melody that was picked out on the other strings.

I knew the song. I'd heard it by the Ganges and played along note-for-note. Very pleased, the old Iban recognised the symbol on my harp and pointed it out to his friends.

We kept playing and the party livened up. More tuak. I liked these people! The rest of the night became a blur of drink, music, dancing and bamboo needles.

Needles?

I was still in my clothes when Raja shook me awake. My head felt like a large, throbbing football, while my hand had swollen to the size of a small one. A fresh tattoo had appeared below the thumb and forefinger. The face in the mirror was a horror.

"Quite a night," said Raja, who didn't look much healthier than I did. "Thank you."

He examined my hand.

"They made you an honorary Iban. You were quite insistent about the tattoo. I couldn't stop you. Better get some shots in KL. But now you've got a plane to catch."

I packed quickly, farewelled my hosts and went out to the car. Freya was already sitting in the front seat. She glared in anger and ignored me all the way to the airport. The driver flashed a knowing smile through his mirror. Men in trouble have a universal bond. Not that it stops schadenfreude when they see a bro in trouble.

Freya stormed out of the car as soon as we stopped at the airport. She loaded up a trolley and wheeled it over to the passenger check-in. The airline clerk directed her to another counter. He gave me the same direction when I followed a minute or two later.

"Please go first to the customs counter."

"Customs? But this a domestic flight."

"Please cooperate with Malaysia's anti-dadah campaign. We have reports of smuggling across the border from Kalimantan, so the government has tightened up on this airport."

Freya was in the queue ahead of me. The customs inspector checked her bags and opened the guitar case. He lifted the instrument out and felt the padding. Freya seemed impatient, but not worried. He held the guitar to his nose, strummed the strings and sniffed.

Slowly the inspector put the instrument down, pulled out a screwdriver and punched a hole in the back. The white powder sandwiched between the two layers of carbon fibre poured onto the counter. He smiled with satisfaction and picked up the phone. Freya stood there impassively until a security guard led her away to the terminal doors. When they slid open, she broke into tears and reached for a tissue.

The young guard relaxed his grip for a second. Long enough for a high kick to the head that sent him flying. Freya leapt through the doorway and escaped before anyone knew what was happening.

A cacophony of sirens and whistles followed. Police and more guards arrived. They sealed off the area, double-checked the passengers and shepherded them onto their flights. A stern voice hurried me along. I boarded the aircraft stunned and confused.

Were they both in on it, or just her? Was it all just one of their games? I had to confront Loki before returning to Melbourne.

My hand was aching badly when we landed in Kuala Lumpur. The airport doctor pumped me full of antibiotics, a tetanus shot and a painkiller. He examined the tattoo and shook his head.

"You know it's permanent."

"I can live with that. It's been coming for some time."

He handed me a packet of small pills.

"Take these. No alcohol."

I felt better by evening and found the mansion Freya had pointed out. The Planter's Bar was decked out with cane chairs, ceiling fans, old photographs and colonial memorabilia. A very Foreign Correspondents Watering Hole. I ordered an Angkor beer and sat near the door to wait for Loki. I had plenty of time until my midnight flight.

The Australian journalist had the attention of his colleagues at a nearby table.

"...and then this blonde, Swedish bird, who's been caught with a stack of smack, lays out the cop with some kind of martial arts kick and scarpers through the crowd at Kuching airport."

"Was that the one with the guitar who looks like the singer from ABBA?" asked the Englishman.

"That's her," said the French correspondent. "Our Stockholm office is going big on this. They say she was some top singer with goddess-like status who threw it all in. Some neo-Nazis beat her husband to death in front of her outside a night-club. She disappeared after that."

"What's the word for pig? Is it *babi*?" asked the Australian. His colleagues nodded. "I can see tomorrow's headlines in the Post." He read aloud from an imaginary newspaper. *"ABBA Dadah Pusher Bashes Babi."*

The others groaned in appreciation. An American woman wearing a black eyepatch joined the group with a round of drinks.

"Norse goddess. Drug smuggler. Kicks her way to freedom. Sounds like a male, middle-aged hack's fantasy. What are you guys doing with your left hand under the table?"

"Don't be like that," retorted the Englishman. He waved a limp left hand and crossed his eyes. "No worse than some of the stuff from your agency. What are you working on?"

"It looks like Swedes are today's hot item. We've got a report from Phnom Penh about a Swedish national found crucified. Chained to a boulder and left for the animals. Something tore his liver out."

"Who was he?" asked the German.

"They're not sure. He was carrying a press pass, but it may have been fake. They think our young Prometheus was caught selling guns to the Montagnards."

"Speaking of Swedes," said the Australian, "whatever happened to that mad bastard who used to pass through here regularly? Never stopped talking and made the drinks disappear."

"You don't suppose...?" said the American. She stopped in mid-sentence at the sound of my glass hitting the floor.

BACK TO EARTH

Carousing students filled the Jumbo charter to Melbourne. They gathered in the aisles to show off souvenirs and swap travel stories. Some were my age, but I felt much older, more detached.

I spent the flight trying to sort out the experiences of the past months—the mentors, the tricksters, the tests. Was I returning with some Elixir of Knowledge, or just the can of Coke in my hand? Did Loki and Freya really live their creed and pay the price? Or had I been set up to carry $100,000 worth of heroin through customs?

Freya was probably floating on some river in Borneo, on her way back to the sea, while Loki had fulfilled Zarathustra's dictum to the dying man: *Now you perish through your calling.* Ironically, Loki's words on betrayal had saved me. Had I not heeded his warning, I would have been carrying the guitar the second time.

Back to earth. The students applauded as the plane bumped down and taxied to the terminal. Two pot-bellied men got on, Gog and Magog, in navy shorts and long white socks, brandishing aerosol cans. Walking up and down the aisles, their arms swayed like cobras. The spray hissed and spat at any evils from the outside world that would dare threaten Australia's purity. The men swaggered off the plane like portly Pied Pipers, followed by a horde of frolicking youngsters.

Another customs inspection. The official checked my passport. The travel pattern was different from the other charter passengers. He muttered something to his partner about a *Red Profile* and began asking questions.

"So why didn't you stay with the ship, Mr. Hunter?"

"I returned to help a sick friend."

He looked at me in mock belief.

"Not a sick mother?"

He searched my pack and extracted the harp.

"Might this be used as a smoking implement?"

"Not unless you want to blow sixteen joints at once."

I wasn't in the mood for this. Neither was he. He pressed a buzzer and led me away to a back room for a strip search. Out came the rubber glove. It's hard to feel like a warrior returning in triumph when you've got an Ansell up your asshole.

"Shouldn't you ask me out for dinner first?"

My friend was still not amused.

"You'd prefer the laxative and shit-bucket special?"

I sensed it was time to shut up. After another search and more questions, I was released, to his obvious disappointment.

The arrival lounge was almost empty by the time I emerged. Thorry and Laszlo were waiting outside the sliding doors. We shook hands and hugged each other, all talking at once. Gary rolled over in his wheelchair. Sibyl stood behind him, holding Jason, who gurgled in contentment. Gary looked up with his familiar grin, but there was no light in his eyes.

"You look different," he said, squeezing my hand.

Sybil hugged me and whispered a thanks in my ear. "Things have already improved since he got your card."

"Great tatt," she said aloud. "You're now initiated."

"Let's eat," said Thorry. "I want to hear all about it."

We squeezed into Gary's station-wagon, parked the wrong way against the gutter. He wheeled up the footpath to the door and swung into the driver's seat. He then folded the chair and manoeuvred it into place behind him.

I didn't know whether to comment on this dexterity or pretend everything was normal. The others were taking these moves for granted so I let it go. I showed my interest in the ingenious throttle and brake hand-lever attached to the steering column.

"Did it myself," said Gary matter-of-factly, hiding the pride he would have normally shown in such an achievement. "At least I can drive now. Sibyl got sick of me just hanging around the house."

She ignored the bait.

"Let's try that new bistro in the pub near our place. They've converted the old blood-house."

"You bought your house at the right time," said Laszlo. "Looks like the area's going upmarket."

"My brother put us onto it," said Sibyl. "He could see it coming."

We let that one go.

It was still early evening when we arrived and the Camelot was nearly empty. The owner welcomed us at the door and introduced himself.

"My name's Dionysus. My friends call me Dion."

He led us to a wooden table and discreetly removed one chair. We placed our orders and I caught up on the past months.

Thorry was happy to be back home with his dog and snowdomes. He was working in the family's carpentry business, but still plagued the neighbours with his drumming. The latest passion was the djembe. He'd enrolled in an African drum class where he met his new girlfriend. The others teased him about quietening down as a result. Laszlo had joined a law practice and resumed his violin studies. Both to the relief of his mother. Sibyl was teaching, while Gary "considered his options."

Two carafes later, we were reminiscing. While everyone now had a regular income, I sensed they missed the excitement of HellHound on the road.

"By the way," I asked casually, "whatever happened to the Three Sisters?"

"Haven't seen them for a long time," said Laszlo. "I heard they toured overseas." An old suspicion returned. "Why do you ask?"

"No reason. No reason."

Dion turned up the stereo behind the bar, to start the party.

"Markos Vamvakaris, the Grandfather of Rembetika," he said.

It triggered a memory.

"You don't happen to have a cousin called Theo who works out west?"

Dion looked at me in surprise.

"Why, yes, I haven't heard from him in ages. Does he still play that old bouzouki?"

Dion grabbed a glass and sat down to join us. His eyes lit up with the story of our music at the mine.

"You know, I'm looking for a good live band here. But something more than the usual pub group you can hear anywhere."

He excused himself to greet some new customers. Jason was restless and signalled it was time to go.

"You're probably tired too," said Sibyl. "The spare room is all ready, for as long as you need it."

We exchanged telephone numbers with Dion and promised to keep in touch. Gary dropped off Laszlo and Thorry on the way to his house. Wheelchair ramps covered all the steps and uneven surfaces of the Victorian terrace. Old HellHound posters lined the passageway. I showered in the converted bathroom, surrounded by flasks, bottles and stainless-steel pans.

Sibyl was putting Jason to bed when I joined Gary in the kitchen. He poured wine into two goblets and handed me one. It was the old goblet found under my bed when we were cleaning out the hut at Corazon.

"Were you looking for this? Thorry gave it to me."

"Not sure if it's worth the trouble."

We drank the red wine.

"So, looking back, what was the highlight of the trip?"

I chose the Thaipusam story for Gary's sake, to make a point about the spirit overcoming the body.

"Marco Polo got it right, way back then," I said at the end. "The West doesn't have all the answers."

"Not if you believe the Single Society Party."

"Who?"

"That's all been happening while you were away. They're running around saying the Asians are going to swamp us."

"Have they got much support?"

"They're feeding on the young and hopeless. Using skinheads to do the dirty work. Could hold the balance of power next election, so the government's too gutless to do anything about it."

"Too gutless or too much in agreement?"

"Maybe both. Anyway, what are your plans?"

"I'm not sure yet. I'll have to find a day job soon. I'm nearly broke again."

"Something coming up next month might interest you. I became friends in hospital with the news editor of Radio Mercury. The SS beat him up because of the stories he ran about them. He's looking for a new crime reporter to train up."

"I've never done anything like that."

"Not exactly. But they want someone who can write, operate on their own and, um, is a bit of a desperado. Sibyl showed him your letters and he said he'd like to talk to you."

"Thanks for thinking of me. I'm flattered. But not so sure about the desperado bit."

"It's worth a call."

Sibyl re-joined us briefly to say goodnight. Gary wheeled to the bathroom to empty his leg-bag.

"Been playing much?" I asked when he returned, even though I knew the answer.

"Nah, gave it away. I tried some of the stuff you suggested. But what's the point? No one wants to see a crip on stage."

"Your son might."

Gary's eyes moistened and he pointed to his wheelchair.

"How can I be a hero to him?"

"What about Sonny Terry and Brownie McGhee? They only had one working pair of legs and eyes between them."

"I'm no Brownie McGhee."

"But at least you're alive."

He stared straight ahead.

"So what?"

"Let me tell you about a couple I met in Calcutta."

I told him about Loki and Freya in full detail, but must have laboured the existential significance of Loki's fate. When I'd finished, Gary looked puzzled, as if pondering a faulty carburetor and downed his drink.

"So, after all that, you didn't even get to screw her!"

I spluttered in astonishment and he started laughing. I joined in and raised my arms in a gesture of mock outrage.

"That's the last time I talk deep and meaningful to you."

"You should have seen the earnest look on your face."

He refilled the goblets.

"I hope you and Sibyl don't mind. I invited the others over for a bit of a blow here tomorrow," I said. "Just for old times' sake. If it goes well, I might even ask Dion for an audition."

Gary's smile faded.

"It'll be good to hear you again. But as I told you, I'm out of it."

The next night, it was apparent we all were. Thorry was in Mali, Laszlo was playing gypsy jazz in the Hot Club of Paris and I was on the banks of the Ganges. Gary sat in the corner pretending not to listen and bounced Jason up and down in time to some other unheard beat.

"You sound all over the place," said Sibyl. "Why don't you try straight blues?"

"Dion is after more than that," I replied. "He wants to hear the world, not only Chicago."

We kept playing, experimenting and trying to blend, but it still sounded like a conversation in three languages, with no one listening.

"We can bring in a keyboard player and horns on the night," said a frustrated Thorry.

"Yes, but they have to play off us. The core sound still has to be there," answered Laszlo.

"We've got the spices and treasures in our saddlebags, but we're like plodding camels. There's nothing driving us to our destination."

I was feeling metaphorical.

"Let's change the tempo," said Thorry and tapped out a quick Egyptian beat.

Laszlo laid down some flamenco chords in Phrygian mode to go with it. I started blowing a song of the desert.

Suddenly, the venetian blinds shook to the low roar of the Sirocco. It enveloped the caravan and swept us along. We turned around, still playing. Gary was plugged in, eyes closed and flying. He cradled his bass awkwardly in the wheelchair. But the sound was strong and defiant. The notes swirled over the sand dunes of North Africa and swept into the Mediterranean.

"Yes!" yelled Thorry, thumping louder, pushing Laszlo and I to play harder. Jason rocked backwards and forwards on his rug, clapping.

"Okay, you bastards, you win," said Gary when the wind died down. "I'm back. You can stop pretending now."

▨▨▨▨▨▨

Sita looks down. We're holding hands. The Camelot is empty. Dion sweeps up broken glass by the bar.

"Well, that was an elaborate answer to a simple question about your tattoo. Was any of it true?"

"It will be when I write it. And besides, a beautiful Muse inspires epics."

Her eyes roll upwards, but her hand stays in mine. I decide to pump up the valiant knight bit not to lose the advantage.

"At least allow me to escort you home on my trusty steed."

"Will I be safe?"

Dion squeezes my arm on the way out. "Jousts aside, you topped yourself tonight." He nods towards Sita with a look that says "take it easy."

I stagger, only slightly, on the way to the car-park. Rain clouds have gathered. Arion stands alone under the security spotlight.

"Very nice," said Sita. "The Custom series. Where did you get it?"

"There's quite a story..."

"Not now." This is not One Thousand and One Nights. She puts her finger to my lips.

I kiss her hand and gesture nobly towards the bike.

"I think I'd better take the reins," she says and holds out her other hand for the keys.

She eases the bike off the stand confidently and straddles it. I resist the temptation to compliment. After all, it's the Seventies. I slide on the pillion seat and clasp her waist.

"No funny business," she half-jokes.

"Sita, the submissive consort—not."

"My mother says there's a touch of Kali there."

"A taste for blood and destruction?"

"Let's say I try to hold my own."

Arion responds well to his new rider. We cruise the quiet streets past a row of terrace houses. A car pulls up and parks. The driver embraces his female passenger and leads her purposefully to the front door. The lights in the hallway and bedroom come on in quick succession.

"That cheating bastard," growls Sita. The bike skids to a halt near a phone box on the corner.

"Friend of yours?"

"Ex-friend. It didn't take him long!" She dismounts and storms into the booth.

"I'll give them a first date to remember!"

The scorned woman dials triple zero, asks for the fire brigade and identifies herself as Mrs. Kali. She sobs the house address, urging the use of pikes and axes to free the hapless residents trapped in the blaze.

The second call is a cry for an ambulance. Pained voice, imminent birth, same address. *Can't get up. Break down the door.* Next up, the police. Extant murder and mayhem. *Bring guns.*

I'm outclassed. Or put on notice?

"Time to go," she says, with a satisfied tone.

"You mean you forgot the emergency numbers for overflowing drains and injured wildlife?"

We speed away to the sounds of three sirens approaching. What a turn-on!

"Do you always invoke the Furies against ex-lovers?"

"Only if they ignore me."

The rains come. Sita softens, appeased. I wrap my jacket around her shoulders.

"Thank you, Sir Knight," she says with a shiver.

We reach the bay and stop in front of a small, ochre house on Ithaca Road.

"I think you need a coffee."

"Just us, or do we share it with the State Emergency Services?"

"Just us," she says with a laugh, and opens the door. The brass, monkey-head knocker winks at me as we walk in.

A HOODED COBRA LIES IN WAIT

The Persian runner leads up the hall into an open area full of furniture, artifacts and wall-hangings from all over Asia. A large window looks out to sea. A bronze figurine of Shiva guards the room from a low wooden table. Encircled by flames and serpents, the Lord of the Dance stands with one leg raised, while the other tramples the evil dwarf.

"Hi Nat, small world."

Sita hangs up my jacket.

Cut to the chase.

"Do you live here alone?"

"Sometimes."

Her hand brushes my shirt.

"You're all wet."

She runs her fingers through my hair. An electric charge runs down my spine. Luckily, I'm earthed.

"I'll be back in a moment."

I wander around to check out the place. A large painting in a carved teak frame dominates a wall. The revelry that awaited Hanuman the Monkey God when he crept into the palace of Ravana, the royal enemy who kidnapped King Rama's wife, Sita.

A book of poetry, written in Sanskrit and English, lies open next to Shiva.

Asleep they lie on cushions of silk brocade
Scattered flowers, clothes in disarray,
Three women, bells on their feet
Play flute, drums and vina.
Another kisses a ruby-studded hookah
And dreams of her lover.
Golden lamplight touches
Ravana's favorite consort.
Under a curved canopy she lingers
Distraught with unsatisfied longing,
A hooded cobra lies in wait.

No wonder Ravana had ten heads.

"Remind you of anything?"

She places a black lacquer tray of Turkish coffee on the table.

"Not recently. But that looks like a great party."

I sip the sweet black brew and look at the painting again.

"Where's Sita in all of this?"

"I'm here."

I put my arms around her and kiss her with all the longing of the painting. And mine.

I breathe her in. My turn to be poetic.

"I can smell the jasmine."

"Hate to say this, but I can smell whiskey, smoke and blood."

"Occupational hazard," I reply, wondering if the mood is broken. Not so, it seems.

"Come with me, Sir Knight and we'll bathe your wounds and serve some Listerine." She leads me by the hand to the bathroom.

Flickering candles light a bath shaped like a giant sea-shell. It rests on a platform decorated with the same ochre, yellow and black floral pattern that borders the painting. She unbuttons my clothes and I descend into the warm, scented water. Sita transforms herself effortlessly into a naked Botticelli Venus and joins me.

We embrace silently. The candlelight dances on the ripples, to the faint sounds of Debussy. I feel reborn.

She gently sponges away the grime of the Road as my hands journey all over her face and body, following every curve.

"It was worth the wait, Sita."

"I was here all the time."

Hours later, the morning sun creeps in and caresses us as we lie entwined among the silk cushions on the divan.

<hr>

The only time we're apart the following months is when I'm on stage playing. The harp never sounded better, inspiring me to reach ever higher. The Camelot is packed out every night. The defeat of Bull-man has made the place famous. But will also lead to its destruction.

Sita and I spend the days on long rides looking for memorable places to drink wine and make love. We live out the Rubaiyat in caves, forests, secluded beaches and a waterfall. My clothes, music sheets and other worldly possessions dutifully join my toothbrush in her temple.

Gary and Sibyl watch with approval as I stuff the remaining items into the bike's saddlebags for the final move.

"About time too," he says.

Sibyl sees me off at the curb.

"You've found her, Chris. Don't blow it."

I pick up Sita and we ride to a park by the Yarra River. We sit under the bough of *our tree*. I try a new piece, called Wild Harp, I've written for the group. A gypsy jazz-swing.

A group of children on a school picnic gather around to listen. I segue to the theme from Sesame Street.

"You'd be good with kids," she says after they leave.

I miss a note. Uh, oh. Trouble in Paradise.

"Maybe, but I don't think I'm ready yet."

"Not just Pan, but Peter Pan as well, it seems."

It's time to go. I have a job interview with the Radio Mercury news editor. I drop Sita off and change. Arion refuses to start when I come out again. I take a green tram to the studios.

Herman, the news editor, peers at me over a thick set of bifocals, giving him multiple sets of eyes. He leaves his desk and walks over with a slight limp to shake hands.

"Yes, I got to know Gary during my stay in rehab. Courtesy of a visit from our friends in Single Society. They didn't like my stories about the Party's terror tactics and shonky finances."

"Do you know who did it?"

"A thug called Yama. Used to be a copper out west. The locals got sick of his bullying and persuaded him to leave. He went even more crazy and the SS snapped him up."

I move uneasily in the chair. We create our own monsters.

"You've heard of him?"

"We've met."

"Anyway, he's but a symptom of a dark cloud I can see descending on this country. The racists and accountants are taking over. That's why we need extra eyes on the news team."

He asks about my travels, reading habits and the journals to Gary.

"I liked the story about your tattoo. There are times you might have to go the limit in this place as well."

"Does that mean I get the job?"

"I'll start you off in the office for a month to let you pick up the basics. Then it's across the river on police rounds. Crime, ambulance chasing and a bit of court reporting."

"Sounds great."

"For a while. But it's unhealthy to stay there too long. Turns you into an old cynic like me. If all that works out, we'll try you out on Argus, our investigative series. There's also the international section."

I can't believe my luck and try to sound casual to hide the excitement.

"What are you working on now?"

"We're looking at military hardware meant for Vietnam, that's finding its way to pirates in Thai and Indonesian waters. The producer wants to hear more about your story."

He looks at the wall of clocks, turns up the hourly bulletin on the desk monitor and stands up.

"You can start here tomorrow."

I rush home to tell Sita the news. She doesn't share my excitement.

"Those four a.m. starts and weekend shifts are not going to be much fun for us."

"It'll also be tricky mixing it with night gigs. But a great opportunity."

"There's something I have to tell you."

"What's up?"

"Dion just rang, pretty upset. Bull-man wanted revenge on the Camelot after our little encounter. He used his party connections to call out the fiscal fiends from the tax department, plus the licensing posse. They closed the place this afternoon."

I sink into a chair. Sita reads my thoughts.

"It wasn't your fault. And after all, it was how we met."

"Do the others know?"

She nods.

"We should organise a wake."

Sita sits nearby and tousles my hair.

"Umm, perhaps not such a good idea. I seem to recall these things can get out of hand. How about just a nice moonlight ride tonight. There's that secluded beach."

"Very tempting. But the bike's been playing up. I'll have to see what's wrong before we can go anywhere."

Winter arrives early. My first morning on police rounds is dark, cold and wet. Real trench coat weather. Sita smiles in her sleep when I kiss her before leaving. A Charon Cab is waiting outside. The sour-faced driver mouths off the whole way about dole bludgers, Asian immigrants and hippie protestors. He declares the police are also useless when we arrive at Russell Street headquarters.

The press rooms are a huddle of gloomy cubicles in the basement. Empty beer cans and hamburger wrappers litter the floor. A faded pinup with curling edges is tucked over a fist hole in a flimsy door.

Radio Mercury's so-called office contains a battered typewriter with missing keys, a battered telephone and a police radio-scanner. My new home away from home. I remove my coat and sit on the wonky chair. The scanner bursts into life with a fanfare of static. A frustrated Car 66 reports back that the recent homicide call was a *malicious false alarm*. Sita's sisters are on duty!

My first job is to check the overnight police reports on noteworthy murders, arsons, robberies and rapes. A dark-eyed Truth & Freedom reporter, sporting a crumpled suit and stained tie, scurries over to the table. In the grimy, neon light he looks like a rat inspecting the carrion of human misery. He sniffs at me indifferently and hands over the clipboard. I jot down some details and call the morning editor with a list of story options for the morning bulletin.

"Chase up that Lazarus shotgun murder first, but hold the details for midday," he barks. "We're getting complaints about running the blood-and-gutsers over breakfast."

I type out the three-par items, wincing every time I hit the sharp lever missing the S key. Talk about suffering for your art. The phone rings.

"Don't forget the Magistrate's Court at ten. Should be a couple of yarns there today."

I dial some follow-up calls and file three pieces. It's a good morning. A Vietnamese family of four living above their shop have died in a fire. *Suspicious circumstances.* A double fatality in an MG sports car given to a 21-year-old the night of his birthday party. *Devastated family blames penny-pinching council for poor road conditions.* And the arrest of Mrs. Mary Lazarus over the shooting of her husband.

I join the other reporters on the Press Bench in the court room across the road. They check their watches during the minor assaults, burglaries and other low-interest cases.

Will Mrs. Lazarus appear in time for the midday news?

At 11:40 a.m., a thin, frightened woman is escorted into the dock. Laid off and dependent on her drunken husband, the court is told. Tired of the nightly assaults, she waited on the couch for his return and allegedly welcomed him with the family shotgun—a Browning semi-automatic. Appropriately, the 12-gauge Anniversary Model. Police found parts of the offending Mr. Lazarus spread around the living-room door, where he tried to escape. The Press Benchers scribble furiously and race to their telephones. Each leads with a variation on *this Lazarus won't be rising from the grave.*

I'm appalled. And miss the deadline. The editor bawls me out, then remembers it's my first day on the round.

"You'll have to try harder tomorrow. Don't let it get to you. Otherwise, you won't last."

I redeem myself in the weeks that follow. There's a lead story about a wire-haired terrier left in a room with a sleeping new-born, just back from hospital. In a jealous fit, Rascal had savaged the baby to death.

An alert photographer arrives at the house in time to catch a close-up of the bloodstained mouth as police lead the dog out of the nursery. Tail wagging. The TV crew also lucks out. The distraught father has to be held down when he tries to snatch a cop's revolver to shoot the family pet. The incident sparks a furious public debate over media responsibility, invasion of privacy and what should be done with Rascal.

I get the heady thrill of my first scoop when an exasperated detective opens up to me in the local pub.

"I've been getting abusive calls from people trying to save the dog's life and saying we've got no right to put it down without a fair trial. They've let a rapist murderer go on a technicality and no one gives a stuff. Yet that bloody animal's become a media celebrity with adoption offers from as far away as California."

It's a dog's life, declaim the editorials quoting my interview. Talkback radio fills with calls that animals should not be condemned for their instincts.

The irregular hours and weekend work take their toll. I spend less time with my friends and start mixing more with the other scribes. A tribe with its own rituals, values and language. Sita notices I'm practising the harp less and spending hours poring over newspaper crime pages.

"Is this what you're giving up your music for? To be a voyeur in Hell?"

"It's only temporary, until I can move on to something better. Besides, the music has no future these days. With the recession, Camelot wasn't the only place to close down. We can't find another gig."

"Is that all your gift means to you? A paid gig? You're changing."

She's right again. It's time to leave the crime beat. The opportunity comes that week during a dinner party. Just as we sit down to Vivaldi and prawn cocktails, the phone rings. The night editor wants me to follow up reports of a grisly murder at Sunshine Towers, a housing development just up the road.

The Department of Community Services had cleared an inner-city neighbourhood to make way for the controversial block—touted as a *cost-effective housing for challenged socio-economic groups*. Sita's furious at the interruption to our first Saturday night together for months So am I when I arrive at the grey, tomb-like edifice.

"You've wasted your time," says a disappointed photographer walking the other way. "False alarm. It was only a sooey." His use of the diminutive emphasises the triviality of the desperate death.

"Hell of a mess though. Someone dived off the roof into the kids' playground and decorated the slide."

I stand on the footpath unsure what to do next. It seems pointless to go back and say there was no story in the mere suicide that ruined our evening.

A young man wearing dark sunglasses taps his way down the pavement with a white stick. He stops in front of me.

"Hi, I'm Ty. The pedestrian lights aren't working. Do you mind helping me across the road?"

Tiresias in jeans and a Four Horsemen T-shirt?

I hold his arm and guide him through the shark pool of heavy traffic to the other side.

"Where are you going? I've got time to take you."

"The Pink Pussycat."

"You're going to a strip-club?"

Ty smarts at the rising inflection.

"There's more than one way of seeing. When you lose one of your senses, the others expand. There's more to experience than the obvious."

I ask no more questions.

"The place you want is a five-minute walk straight ahead. You'll hear it."

"More than that. Thanks, I can find it myself now."

His face lights up in anticipation as he taps away.

Is our meeting a guiding message to go beyond the obvious? I cross the road again for a closer look at Sunshine Towers. An ambulance drives by with red light flashing, as if it would make a difference to the occupant. I wander around the bleak 25-storey building. Two years old and the walls are already cracking. Two women are playing *I told you so* in a doorway.

"Maybe now they'll put a higher fence around the roof."

"That's the third jump this month."

"Not to mention that old lady who died all alone in Block Two. It was three weeks before they found her. All stiff."

"I heard they had to wrap her in garbage bags and carry her out upright. The elevators are too small for a stretcher."

I rewind my cassette recorder, walk over and identify myself. The women are only too willing to talk about Sunshine life. They introduce me to neighbours with their own tales of The Horror.

What emerges is a massively botched public project with all decisions based on cost rather than need. The frail and elderly were often trapped in the top floors because the elevators kept breaking down. It took weeks to get them repaired and the old lady had starved to death.

Syringes and broken bottles barred use of the playground. Teenage gangs preyed at night on passers-by in a project that had *cost-effectively* concentrated the sick, the poor and the unemployed in a high-rise, low-rent ghetto.

I race back to the studio and cut the interviews into a documentary called The Dark Shadows of Sunshine Towers. The program causes outrage. An official inquiry condemns the unpopular complex and the residents are relocated. The government loses crucial inner-suburban seats at elections a week later and the program wins an award.

No more police rounds, a promotion to Radio Mercury's international section and apparent proof that the word has more power to heal than music. I am to learn that the word also has more power to lie.

AMIGO DE XANGO

Cristo Redentor looks out over Rio with arms outstretched in the spotlights. Corcovado's concrete reminder that there's hope in Art Deco for us all. I descend the mountain curves on a rented Xango 1100. It roars like the eponymous lord of thunder. An imaginary Sita rides with me.

"You've been neglected lately. I promise to make amends when I return. But look where I finally am!"

The road flattens out and I cruise through the tunnel to Copacabana. The steady rhythm of the engine shifts into a drumbeat that echoes off the walls.

Avenida Atlantica. The drumbeat gets louder. The rhythm that entered my dreams so long ago and flowed through everything I played after that. I park the bike under a palm tree on the undulating black and white walkway. The beach is crowded with New Year's Eve revellers.

Where am I going? I feel guided by an outside force.

Devotees of Umbanda gather on the sand beside bonfires and candles. They swirl to the mesmerising percussion of the ganzá, afoxé and cuica, riding on the booming, bass surdo. The sounds of ancient Africa. Votive candles illuminate mystical symbols inscribed on the sand. They come alive and dance with shadows that flicker in tempo.

Twelve people dressed in white circle a large, blazing cross. A devotion seared with the memory of the five million slaves who died on the way to Brazil. And the blessing of the red-hot iron cross that branded those who survived.

Further down the beach an entranced medium sways in front of an effigy, summoning the goddess from her astral realm. An open bottle of cachaca spirit stands on a large flat rock that serves as the altar. Seven candles surround it. The memory returns.

So that's what happened! I had to fly to Rio in person to find out.

A million voices chant the countdown to midnight and the celebrants rush to the water's edge. They launch small candle-lit boats and other offerings to supplicate Yemanja's favour for the coming year.

I look out to sea. The moon is reflected in a million ripples. A figure with long dark hair dances across the water in her light blue robes. Fan in one hand and a short scimitar in the other. Relief and retribution. She pauses a moment, looks at me and raises the curved blade in warning. The dance continues. I sit amongst the crowd with my feet in the water, waiting for the sunrise.

I've arrived at the source. The saints, the gods, the nymphs, the warriors and the music have all come together in Brazil. Xango as Thor as Saint Jerome. Oxum as Saint Bartholomew as Shiva dancing through the cosmos with snakes. Ogun, like Vulcan, a blacksmith.

I've found the life force that keeps the fantasy alive. Just before I let the flame die out.

I watch the sun rise slowly from the sea to ignite the sky. The ritual is over for another year. Half-dazed I wander back to the bike to ride off in the golden light.

At a downtown intersection, near the Freedom International Office, I'm stopped by a military check-point. A reminder of why I was sent to Brazil. The captain lowers his revolver and demands my ID papers with cold, official politeness.

"Por favor me mostre sua carteira de identificação."

His four men hold their automatics ready. One of them searches through my shoulder bag. Just as well Herman had insisted I take a tape-recorder that looks like an innocuous Walkman.

The captain flicks open the lid and plays the first few seconds of a cassette labelled Meditation for Motorcyclists. He switches the recorder off, just before the tape reaches my interview with a wanted dissident. I gesture to the guards that staring down a gun-barrel is not conducive to inner peace. It really isn't.

I look around for a distraction. An open bottle of cachaça, a cigar and a box of matches have been arranged by the crossroads. Hopefully they'll placate more than the spirits in the area.

The captain asks questions in Portuguese I can't understand.

"Turista," I reply waving my passport. He checks it again, spots my tattoo and stops.

"Okay," he says in recognition and waves me on.

After a roadside breakfast of pingado and pão na chapa, I arrive at the Paraiso Hotel for the key interview of my Brazil assignment. I take the elevator to the penthouse. A burly butler opens the door and escorts me inside. Through the window, Sugar Loaf Peak oversees the entrance to Guanabara Bay. The water shimmers in the morning light against a backdrop of purple mountains. Hang-gliders hover around the hotel like guardian angels.

Urbane, persuasive and friend to every dictator in the region, Dolos sits waiting. His white shirt and trousers render him almost invisible against the white couch and walls. Herman had warned me to keep my distance.

"Congratulations, Chris Hunter, you've lived up to both parts of your name. Assuming it's real."

He pours black coffee from the silver pot, engraved with an evil eye.

"How did you find me?"

"You left a golden trail to Rio. After that, I just had to ask for the best pub in town."

He shrugs in mock helplessness and we size each other up.

"What made you think I'd agree to the interview?"

"The opportunity to give your side of the story. Without the necessity of appearing in court."

"That's unlikely. Don't believe the reports. Apart from anything else, they show an ignorance of standard international business practice."

"Standard practice? Would you have done deals with Nazi Germany?"

He reflects for a moment.

"It would have been tricky after 1938."

"Reports claim you're dealing with descendants of those that flourished in that period."

"Media nonsense. Where's the proof?"

"There's proof that some of your present political contacts are just as brutal as their Third Reich role-models."

"That's an internal political issue. If you refused to deal with a country because you disapproved of the government, you wouldn't do business with anyone. How many trade embargoes did you see imposed on the US by those who disapproved of Vietnam?"

"Does that make it right?"

"Who's to say what's right?"

"And the Amazon rainforests?"

"A simple commercial decision. They're worth more as cattle pastures."

"For junky hamburgers."

He sighs, walks to the window and gestures.

"Look that way and you'll see the world's best view. After Sydney Harbour of course! Look the other way and you'll see the favelas—some of the world's most desperate slums. I'm helping them on the road to development."

"A road that includes death squads, torture and sweat-shops for a dollar a day."

"It cuts both ways. Don't forget the recent slaughter of the Yanomani Indians by desperate goldminers. Poverty affects everyone. Isolating these countries won't make it better."

"Supporting corrupt rulers will?"

"Sounds like you've been talking to the Liberation Missionaries."

"Of whom you don't approve?"

"Tools of the Marxists."

"The Vatican is right to condemn them?"

"It's easy to stir up the slums. I suppose that's the location of your next interview. For ironic contrast."

"You should have been a journalist."

"I was. And more. In fact, my company's going to take over yours."

He sits down on a chair by a small table, black, piercing eyes fixed on mine. This is not going well. I stare down and notice a framed photo of a blonde-haired woman performing a roundhouse kick in mid-air.

"A fine example of the armada pulada by my favourite capoerista," says Dolos.

"Freya's been very helpful since she arrived here. Brazil's limits on extradition benefit a wide range of people."

I try to stop the gasp.

"Interested? I could arrange a meeting if you like. By the way, how's your home life?"

That one hurts. I'm not keeping my distance.

"You're a busy man. I think we should get some of this down."

He nods victoriously. I press the record button and set the level.

"Mr. Dolos, how do you respond to accusations that your business dealings in South America are helping to prop up brutal regimes?"

The sparring continues on tape for half-an-hour until the cassette clicks off. He looks at his gold Rolex watch to signal the interview is over. I check the recording and pack my gear. Dolos walks me to the entrance.

"It's not as black-and-white as you're making out. They recognise that here. Even their favourite gods have a dark side. You, of all people, should be able to recognise that."

He shakes my hand with an overpowering grip.

"And please spell Dolos correctly."

"As in the god of trickery?"

"Or alternate reality."

The door closes.

I ride down with a hollow feeling, as if I've left something behind in the penthouse.

Dolos is right about the next interview, lined up with an Australian missionary working amongst Rio's poor. His parish is easy to find. At the end of the street, I follow a muddy path, strewn with rubbish. It stinks of sewage. The path leads to a collection of hillside shacks built from planks, rusted iron sheets and rough clay bricks.

Dolos was also right about the favelas providing ironic contrast. The country's richest and the poorest share the same view. I pass some children playing happily in a scrap heap. A perfect symbol. Their joyful innocence amongst life's detritus will be my opening para.

An old woman staggers up the steep makeshift steps. She pants under a heavy container. Tears well up in her eyes. I offer to carry the water and lift it to my shoulder. She accepts with surprise and gratitude. I follow her to a tumbledown hut.

"Obrigado, senhor!"

"Seja bem-vinda!"

Perhaps she knows where the missionary lives.

"Estou procurando um missionário Australiano, Padre Brian?"

She nods and crosses her wrists as if in manacles. I guess that means the interview will have to wait.

"A policia prendeu ele. Foi deportado."

She points back down the steps and signals that I should also leave. I pretend not to understand and walk off. At least I can get some background.

I take out the camera. Big mistake. Hostile looks remind me this is not a press conference in Melbourne. A group of teenage boys circles. I pretend to ignore them. Two of the gang pull out knives and flip them with practised ease.

Another time, I might have distracted them with music. Charmed the beasts like Larry Adler did with Al Capone and Legs Diamond. It had worked before. I reflexively reach for my harp, forgetting I've left it behind. I don't play it much these days. A tape-recorder and camera are my new talismans—minus the magic.

The gang closes in, knives arcing.

"Não, não faça issam!"

The old woman runs up and pulls back three of the boys, asserting her familiarity with them.

"Não, Gilberto! Não, Jorge! Não, Caetano!"

They respond out of respect, but are unhappy with the prospect of losing their quarry. The leader argues with her, pointing to my watch and camera. The woman takes my hand to show I'm her friend.

"Ele é meu amigo."

She points to the tattoo, suggesting I also have friends in higher places.

"Olhem, ele é amigo do Xangô."

The power is fading, but sways the argument. The boys grudgingly allow her to lead me away to the trolley station.

"Muito obrigado, senhora."

"Seja bem-vindo!"

She lifts my hand, looks at it again and makes a parting comment that sounds like occupar-se de Oxum. Something about looking after Oxum.

I return to the hotel and attack the mini-bar. A telex message slides under the door.

> Series excellent, but forget Dolos story.
> Return soonest. Radio Mercury taken
> over in corporate merger. Many changes.
> Herman.

"Who's Oxum?" I ask the receptionist, when checking out.

She gives me a knowing smile.

"Goddess of the river. Xango's second wife."

"What's special about her?"

"She's known for her elegance and beauty. But she also has a dark side and can be malicious."

A FALSE GOD

I write up all my stories and interviews on the long flight back. When finished, I lean back in the chair to think about the future of my career. Is it all worthwhile? I can't sleep. Reading the inflight magazine might help.

Amidst the luxury watch ads and vapid resort promos is a travel feature about a free-diving competition off Sardinia. Divers without air-tanks risk blackouts and hallucinations to stay underwater for more than ten minutes on one breath. Some descend an astounding seven hundred feet using a breathing technique that reminds me of one from Apollo. I wonder if I'll ever need it again?

I switch off the reading light and doze with troubling memories of the meeting with Dolos and the warning about Oxum.

Sita greets me at the airport, ready for the road, looking like a rock star ninja in her black riding outfit. The jet lag melts away. We hug before speaking, but I sense a hesitancy on her part. This time I've been away too long.

"I got your messages, Chris. Did you miss me?"

"I want to show you how much."

"I can't imagine what you have in mind."

Arion sits outside, gleaming and tuned.

"We've been waiting for you."

She hands me a black leather jacket.

"Your armour, Sir Knight."

We hit the freeway and head for the bay in the warm, night breeze.

I turn to her at a red light.

"Sita, I want to start again. I want to show you where it all began. In Brazil, I think I found the key to the mystery. And I want you to unlock it with me."

Her arms tighten around me in anticipation.

"But we'll have to stop at a supermarket first."

"Who would have thought that the journey to revelation starts at Safeway?"

I pull up at the main door and leave Sita on the bike, engine running.

"This won't take long."

The supermarket sound system is playing insipid string versions of tango favourites, interrupted by announcements that Dri Bots Baby Wipes are on special. I grab what I want and stand in the checkout queue behind a tired-looking woman in a track suit and sheepskin slippers. She scolds a toddler for pulling chocolates off the stand. Her husband slouches over the shopping trolley. He raises his eyebrows at me in bored resignation. I can't wait to get outside.

The coast road takes us south to Seaford and the turn-off at the Avalon Milk Bar. We stop at Kananook Creek and I park Arion near the site of the old battleground. Some kids have built a fort on the bank, as if I had never left.

"This was where I found the harp. The start of the journey, when I was twelve."

"I remember the place."

We walk over to the large, flat boulder. I take seven candles out of the plastic bag and place them on top. I light the candles and open a bottle of Bacchus Reserve Hermitage. Sita has already spread out the rug. We drink the wine and talk about the time I was away.

"Did my friends look after you?"

"There was no need, but Laszlo dropped in occasionally to make sure everything was okay."

No response. I'm too engrossed marking the sand with a symbol I saw near the effigy of Yemanja.

"Play something from Brazil."

"How about a saudade I heard on the beach?"

"A saudade?"

"I think you know. It's their blues. A happy sadness against the odds. A yearning for someone."

"Was that how you were feeling?"

"Yes, but I could also feel you with me sometimes."

"You mean, in my old lady disguise?"

She leans against me as I play. The harp sings as if making up for the long neglect. The timeless melody drifts through the reeds and trees, along the flowing water. It continues after I place the harp on the rock and our bodies touch. As if it were the first time. It's just as I had imagined all those years ago.

I reach for the small packet. Sita stops me.

"Chris, I want us to have a child. This is the perfect night to create one."

I freeze. I'm still not ready. I want to travel on with Mercury. To ride with the gods again. To avoid Safeway. The seven candles flicker in the breeze and their light goes out. I move away from Sita. She lets out a cry. The same sound as the water-hen killed by a wanton young warrior with a slingshot.

"You don't want to grow up. You just want to keep flying around in your Never-Never Land with me as your little fairy, fluttering around."

She gets up and dresses hurriedly. Her hand knocks the harp back down the deep hole in the rock. This time I can't reach it. A sharp edge cuts a stigmata across the tattoo on the back of my hand. Blood drips as I follow Sita back to the bike. We ride home in silence. Sitting apart.

The night is a return to the beginning. And the end.

I wake up the next morning to a stony Medusa stare.

"We have to talk."

The dreaded phrase that ranks with "what are you thinking?" and "I've bought tickets to the opera."

I raise my crucified hand. The blood has seeped through the bandage.

No sympathy. This could be serious.

"What was happening there?" she demands "Your tacky sixties fantasy?"

My move: righteous indignation.

"I regret I ever told you about that."

"Well, you did have one or two drinks too many, that night."

Pause for dramatic effect.

"As usual."

I get out of bed. No point hanging around a disaster zone. Sita is already dressed. She sits by the mirror and brushes her long, dark hair angrily. We're playing the destructive coda to a dying melody. The descent into the emotional underworld.

I turn away and walk to the window. The house on Ithaca Road faces the stormy bay. Metal rigging clatters on restless boats moored in the wine-dark sea.

My move.

"I guess it hasn't been as much fun since I took a different path."

"That's an understatement. You don't live in reality. I'm not some goddess inside your mental mishmash of mythomania."

Ouch! Alliteration as a domestic weapon. Obviously prepared.

"You've wasted your gift. Even when you're here and not working, your mind's elsewhere."

I raise the white flag.

"Can we give it one more try?"

"We've been through it all before. Last night was the finish."

Her voice hardens.

"However, you won't be here tonight, in my house, when I return. Bon voyage, Chris."

I look back, but this Orpheus has lost his Eurydice.

I walk to the bed and sit down. Not so invincible now. The alarm clock on the floor signals the bout is over. It also reminds me I have a meeting with the editor. I dress and pack my stuff. It won't take long. As the song says, I'm travelling light.

I scoop up a white wreath of sheet music lying on the table. A Polaroid snap falls out. Taken the night we met, two smiling people in leather jackets hold hands across a table. Between them stands a bottle and three empty glasses. I pick up the picture and see it again for the first time. Fadeout to memory.

My arrival at Radio Mercury is just as joyless. A man with a round, baby face is sitting at a beige desk behind a computer. On the wall, a framed MBA has displaced Herman's Walkley Award for Investigative Journalism.

"Ah good. We've been waiting for your return to conclude the restructuring process."

"Where's Herman?"

"The organisational challenges of the Dolos merger required resource allocation modifications to facilitate new implementation targets."

"You sacked him?"

"He was counselled to re-deploy his skills."

"Herman was nearly crippled getting stories for this place."

"It's no longer cost-effective to maintain previous human resource levels. We're gaining efficiencies by right-sizing and using outsourced, syndicated material."

"What the fuck are you talking about?"

Baby-face becomes serious.

"Don't say anything you might regret. Organisational paradigms are changing. You're a skilled media resource. A content provider with your level of output will help facilitate optimal performance for the company."

"You mean I'm cheap."

"That requires further cost-effective monitoring. Our consultancy division has secured the PR contract for the International Defence Exhibition. They need someone to coordinate publicity outcomes and positive media inputs regarding the high-tech hardware on sale."

"I've stopped playing with slingshots."

"I'm not sure what you mean, but it's that or nothing. You have until the next financial cycle to decide. You'll find there's not much else around these days. Now, if you'll excuse me, I have to progress this assessment report."

He turns back to his screen.

"Oh, and please seek medical attention for your hand. Your blood is staining the carpet."

I shuffle to the door as a man who has sacrificed all to a false god.

THE BLUR

Midday in the cramped city apartment. No reason to get up. The only view from here is a pile of dirty dishes next to a sink half-filled with greasy water. The Scylla and Charybdis of bachelorhood.

The doorbell rings, followed by a heavy thumping when I take too long to answer. I pick up my jeans from the floor and pull them on. It's Dion, smile and banter masking concern. He's holding a scuffed backpack.

"Time to get up, you lazy bastard. You can't stay in there all your life."

He barges in against my protests and looks for two mould-free cups.

"Where's the coffee?"

He sniffs the open milk carton with caution and decides on a strong black brew instead. Dion has lost weight, the midnight pallor is gone and his Woolworth's track suit looks well used.

"Bankruptcy suits you."

"It has its upside. I think I've found my calling. With the hotel gone, there's more time to frolic in the wilderness."

He hands me a cup.

"I can't say the same for you. Check out Dorian Gray in the mirror. Your phone doesn't work?"

"I needed some time alone. I've really blown it."

He holds my shoulder. His eyes look through me.

"We all fall. You'll come to terms with the loss of Sita in your own way. And rise again."

"I've lost more than her."

We drink our coffee silently.

"She's with Laszlo, isn't she?"

"Did you really expect her to stay home weaving patiently, like some Penelope?"

"She gave me a last chance."

"And you made your choice."

He clears a space on the table and puts down the cup.

"We're going after mussels. I've found a great diving spot near Arthur's Seat. We'll polish them off with a great bottle of red I saved from the auditors."

"I don't have any gear."

"No excuse." He pats the pack. "Extra mask, snorkel and flippers that should fit. Size M for Melancholic."

He throws me a crumpled shirt, looks around for two boots that match and marches me outside. A grimy and neglected Arion roars gratefully to life and strains to get through the city onto the highway again. We ride for an hour to the Mornington Peninsula. Dion savours the sea breeze, like a vintage wine from his old cellar.

We pass a small inlet and he shouts directions. We turn off the highway onto a back road.

"Not many people know this place. We have to go through a private property to get there. We're lucky. It was closed off until the farmer went bust and left."

"Do I get the dark-clouds-silver-linings spiel next?"

"Take the dirt road until you see a hole in the fence." He taps my shoulder and points.

"That's it!"

We squeeze Arion through the broken fence and ride across a grassy paddock to the cliff top. We leave the bike and scramble down a steep, overgrown path to the deserted beach. A sharp, foreboding peak stands on a rocky outcrop, casting a shadow across a large rock pool. Beyond the rock, the open sea sparkles in the sunlight. My mood lifts.

"This place is magic, Dion. Why haven't I been here before?"

"Perhaps you have."

We throw off our clothes and dive into the rock pool. Dion splashes around like a child, exulting in the freedom.

"When I come here, the present disappears. I feel like I'm evolving back into innocence. Nothing exists except the senses."

I feel different. I'm in the shadow and the water is cold.

"How deep is it?"

"I'm not sure. There's supposed to be a cave at the bottom with a passage leading out to the sea."

I estimate the distance.

"Let's try it."

"No, you need scuba. It's too far under for one breath. You could run out of air in the tunnel."

The sea beckons in the distance. It challenges me with a choice: to stay in the shadow the rest of my life, confined to a rocky pool. Or to take the risk and strive for the warm open waters. It's the third crossing of the lifeline.

Dion has returned to the rocks for his fishing knife and a sack.

"I'm going to try it, Dion. Wait for me on the other side."

"Don't be crazy. Anything could happen down there."

I inhale and exhale deeply seven times, then another seven, expelling the carbon dioxide from my lungs. With it goes the desire to breathe.

I'll learn in some future life how Dion raced over and dived after me, but I was already too deep. He'll tell how he swam back to the rocks and clambered to the other side of the outcrop. How he looked into the open sea and saw nothing.

A minute will pass. A minute that feels like twenty years.

An eternity later, a naked figure will rise to the surface, as if the ocean had given birth. Dion will deliver it to the shore.

<hr>

Down, down the rocky wall I dive, to the bottom of the pool. I stop to clear my ears and look up. The light is a fading memory and I have entered a silence. Floating, flying. The cave appears, peaceful and inviting. It opens into an immense underwater cathedral, with a flat stone altar in the middle. Strange shapes and shadows dance and merge in the blue light. Is that a sea-nymph sitting on the altar with dark tresses caressing her body?

She casts her green eyes over me and opens her arms.

"Join me. Leave the other world and spend eternity here." We swim around each other, playing like dolphins. The cathedral fills with music. Joyous violins sing paeans to our imminent union. We embrace and I hear the sweet sounds of Vivaldi's *Spring*.

I stop. A memory remains. An atom of carbon dioxide not exhaled. *The Four Seasons*! The staple background of dinner parties dominated by talk of property prices and renovations. Life before and after the extension. Tirades against tradesmen.

What if this be eternity?

I have to breathe again. I push the nymph away.

"You'll be sorry for this," she says.

I fight my way through the tunnel to the sea. To a life of chronic ordinariness that rushes by in a fast forward blur.

A blur of marriages, motor mowers, malls and meetings... suit lapels and ties that grow, shrink and grow again... you'll have to give up drinking... the garbage bin is wheeled out a thousand times... welcome to the company... Safeway specials... For Sale: motorbike and record collection... press releases... Sita returned to India... Laszlo went mad, alone... Thorry became a property developer... Gary and Sibyl have a flower stall at the Queen Vic market.

Head spinning, I reach the end of the tunnel, struggle to the surface and black out.

'WE LIVE IN TWO REALITIES'

I wake up in a strange house wearing checked flannel pyjamas. My back aches and I'm dying for a pee. I walk to the bathroom and glance at the mirror. What's happened? The lined face is familiar, but the hair is thinning and flecked with grey. I look into the eyes. They've dimmed.

How did the man who strove with gods end up in a Paradise Estate semi-detached? The last twenty years have just been a dream. My arms and legs are out of control. I respond like a marionette pulled by the invisible strings of routine. A kitsch Venus de Milo statue watches impassively from the untended garden. Water spouts from a hole in her mouth.

The paper is brought in, the coffee is made, I shave and shower. What next? A diary on the table says *11:00 a.m.: Ministry of Development, Canberra.* An airline ticket and a set of keys beside the diary are clues.

I get dressed and go outside. The keys fit a light blue Cedric sedan that feels familiar. I drive to the airport, present the ticket and catch a plane. My diary shows I have visited Canberra previously for project consultancy. Whatever that is. From the air, the sight of the city's planned, geometric layout stirs vague memories of a different era.

The Greek taxi driver is a prophet of doom. *Business is bad. The city is dying. A wasteland of recession. Government cutbacks. Thousands laid off. Lunatics in the Senate. The Far Right is taking over.*

The taxi stops outside a grey fortress. Another monument to concrete brutalism.

"Help us," says the driver.

A woman in a military-style blazer guides me through the colour-coded corridors past the work-stations for cyber-slaves. Many of the booths are empty. We enter the Serious Executive Board Room. Seven men in dark navy suits, white shirts and red ties are waiting. They brief me in turn.

"Tourism is down and real estate is dropping."

"We need a strategic plan to promote the city."

"Our surveys show the national capital is considered boring and soulless."

"Even the annual flower festival is failing to attract crowds."

"We need a new image."

"Perhaps you can find a historical angle. The archives are all yours."

"We look forward to your proposal in two weeks."

The woman escorts me to a basement full of dusty files. I'm left in a cubicle with a sultana bun and a tepid coffee in a paper cup. The bread and water of the office prisoner.

"Call me if you need anything."

I work my way through the files for two depressing days. Will I rise on the third? Each sliding shelf is a monument to folly, wasted effort, obsession with meaningless ritual.

Multi-million dollar inquiries repeat identical findings and lie unread. Others have been shelved because they didn't support that week's political needs or economic dogma. Tons of minutes, memos, white papers, green papers, committee decisions. A world of weasel words with more visions and missions than the Old Testament. The new corporate church.

My eyes glaze over as I read the ponderous headings and sub-headings, divided by a colon promising a clarification that never appears.

Maximisation of Resource Allocation: Towards a Strategic Plan for Optimal Multi-Skilling.

I sigh and pull out another folder. It contains a report, without the proper reference number. It must have been misfiled. By accident or design? Who cares? I am about to replace the folder when the unusual, colon-less title catches my attention.

The Secret Soul of Canberra.

Attached is a bureaucrat's memo consigning the report to the oblivion of *future consideration* because:

- it promotes a controversial, multicultural interpretation of the national capital's design;

- it equates Aboriginal beliefs with the world's great religions; and hence

- it could provoke objections from the Single Society Party.

A dormant anger ignites with the reference to the SS Party. Bull-man still haunts the labyrinth of officialdom and the government provides him with human sacrifices.

The report's author, Professor Laertes, describes "mystical and religious influences on Walter Burley Griffin and his wife Marion, which shaped their vision for Canberra."

What sort of heretical vision is this? I am moved to read on.

According to Laertes, the original 1912 design shares the planning traditions of ancient capitals such as Rome, Delhi, Babylon and Jerusalem. The city's water and land layout accord with feng shui principles. Despite changes by later planners, the design still reflects early 20th-century eclectic religions, such as Theosophy.

Sceptical, but fascinated, I can see why the report was "lost," especially when I reach the next section. It's about the first inhabitants of the land on which Canberra was built:

> The creation legends of the Aboriginal Dreamtime associated with Canberra's site are represented in the city's geomantic design. The design is based on a sacred symbol, called the Vesica, found in all ancient mythologies. The following page shows a Vesica superimposed on the map of Canberra.

New Age nonsense, I scoff. I turn the page to look at a diagram of the Vesica and freeze.

The faded tattoo on my hand!

I put down the report and lean back in the chair. Here in the dusty basement, I have been given an insight into my other life. The sign was a guide and protector on the Road, before it became a stigma during The Blur.

Oh yes, of course I regret it. The silly things you do when you're young.

I need to know more. The rest of the day is spent calling universities and government departments to track down Professor Laertes. No one can help. A former assistant thinks he's living in the bush somewhere.

"Laertes took off years ago. They suppressed his Canberra research. It was creating political problems. Then his son disappeared."

I remember the disappointment as a boy when my efforts to contact the Apollo School of Music proved just as fruitless. This time I must find him. I look through the report again. No addresses or contact details. There must be a clue somewhere.

The map shows five Canberra peaks supposed to reflect the *Five Sacred Mountains* in feng shui. It connects them to Bimberi Peak, south of the city, the equivalent of Canberra's Mount Olympus. The home of the gods. There, if anywhere.

I rent a car the next day and drive to the bush, past the sheep and cattle farms on the capital's outskirts. The high peak is surrounded by a wilderness reserve far from the highway. I drive around the back roads in the area without really knowing what I'm looking for. The tank is nearly empty, so I head for the mountain village of Adaminaby.

The general store has a petrol pump out the front. A teenager is restoring an old black van parked on the driveway. The name *Jubal* is painted on the side—the father of harp and flute players. I talk to the owner over a coffee inside the store. He's lived in the area for years and knows everyone. I say I'm looking for a lost relative.

"Does anyone live on the mountain?"

"The Aborigines used it for summer festivals, but not much happens there these days."

Frustrated, I pay the bill and ask for the quickest way back to Canberra. But the owner is lost in thought and does not respond with directions.

"Hang on. They say there's some eccentric bloke who built a funny hut up there. Can't remember his name. Although Bimberi's a national park, he took on the bureaucrats with an old title and got away with it."

"Do you know where?"

"Can't help you. It's a large area. He could be anywhere."

I sit in the car and look at the report again. Where would he live? I trace the Vesica's shape on the map. The two central lines form a cross near the peak of Bimberi. I return to the reserve and drive up a little-used dirt road until I reach a locked boom gate. I leave the car and look around. Single tyre-marks show a motorbike has bypassed the gate. The trail leads over a bank to a small track that disappears up the mountain.

I follow the track for three hours. It winds past a grassy fen, down a frost hollow and through creeks and ridges thick with snow-gums. It's a long, hot hike and I'm not as fit as I used to be. The steep track flattens out. I pass through a thicket of wind-ravaged trees and arrive at a small clearing just below the peak. The house of weathered timber and rocks is shaped like a Zen traveller's temple.

Soaring high above
A wedge-tailed eagle shows me
The search has ended.

A silver-haired man wearing a battered Akubra hat and patched jeans is out the front, tuning a motor-bike. He straightens up when he sees me. His height, build and features are similar to mine. He looks like the father I never had.

Laertes?

We shake hands and he embraces me briefly, as if it were a reunion.

"It's taken you a long time to get here."

Laertes is not one for small talk.

"I lost the way," I reply. "Not until we are lost, do we begin to find ourselves."

"Roads were made for journeys, not destinations," he parries.

I didn't think this encounter would end up as an exchange of Taoist aphorisms. But I play along, hoping we'll reach the moment of enlightenment.

"You mean there's no point seeking?"

"The answer was inside you all the time."

"What about Nat, Loki, Theo, all the others I learned from. I had to travel far to find them."

"They were all part of you. Even Dolos."

"The Road is an illusion?"

"You travelled the world, but found and lost Sita in your own backyard. Every day in our own street we pass the mentor, the deceiver, the goddess, the shaman. Waiting to test us, love us, guide us. We don't see them."

"I don't understand."

"We live in two realities—the mundane and the mythical. One is a gift. But we learn to deny it. We neglect our Muse, while searching for her. That's why you ended up here."

This is not the meeting I hoped for. But perhaps it's the only one we could have had. Nevertheless, I feel like I'm Dorothy meeting the Wizard of Oz.

I decide it's time for the Big Question and point to my tattoo.

"Laertes, who am I?"

Like a Michelangelo fresco, he reaches out and touches my hand with a bent finger.

"Who do you want to be? We don't choose where we come from, but we can choose where we go from here."

That's it???

He waits silently for my response. I think about what I learned on the Road and my exile in The Blur.

The answer comes.

"I want my Muse back, so I can finish your work."

Laertes nods and smiles.

"You know what to do."

He turns and walks into his temple. There's nothing more to say. I head back down the track.

⁜

I confront the Seven Suits in their fortress. They close their copies of my proposal and discard them on the table. They need convincing.

"It would be an innovative marketing and investment opportunity to promote Canberra as one of the great capitals of the ancient world, but how can you claim that?"

"There's evidence the city's design shares the same ancient plan, based on the Vesica, with a north-south land axis and an east-west water axis. Even Parliament House sits in a feng shui landscape complete with *White Tiger* and *Azure Dragon*."

"The Chinese delegation in town would like to hear that," jokes one Suit.

"And the Egyptian trade minister would be interested in the comparison of Canberra's layout with the pyramids," adds another. "I'm sure the British Council would go for the Stonehenge parallels."

"How is this linked to Aboriginal myths?"

"The Griffins found all ancient philosophies share a Dreamtime or Golden Age. A time when the world took shape through plants, animals, landforms and people transforming into each other. Canberra sits on land full of ancient stories shared by cultures around the world. The Vesica symbol touches them all."

"Very interesting, but how do we use this to promote tourism and leverage bottom-line outcomes?"

"It's in the proposal. For starters, we organise a festival with exhibitions and performances celebrating all the cultures that influenced Canberra's design. We show that the national capital has an ancient soul. The myths and concepts that compose it are brought together at a World Music festival by the water."

"The government may deem further consideration of this proposal inappropriate, given current, er, negotiations with the Single Society Party."

"The tide is turning. The party now holds the balance of power with only one seat. A festival showing popular opposition to its bigoted views could kill off SS at the next elections."

"And if it doesn't?"

I decide to push the issue. Nothing to lose.

"You hired me because this town has an image problem. What would happen if the media found out that Canberra refused to raise its international profile because the government feared loss of the racist vote?"

The Suits look at each other, then turn to me again.

I go all in.

"And the irony won't be lost that your office is in a building named after Edmund Barton, the father of the White Australia immigration policy. Our regional neighbours won't be impressed.

The Suits shuffle uncomfortably and murmur to each other.

Suit #1 speaks.

"How do we know you can make it happen?"

"Trust me. I'm a consultant. The gods are with us."

He signs the approval.

"We might as well try it. The flower festival's not working. And I'm late for a meeting on Asian trade barriers."

He walks towards the door and turns.

"We'll crucify you if this flops."

▮▮▮▮▮▮▮▮▮

Midnight. Lake Burley Griffin. Commonwealth Park is packed out for the final concert. The culmination of months of hard work and political battles. Canberra has come alive with parades, exhibitions, dancers and performers from all over the world. Package tours of the *Cosmic Capital* are fully booked and the city has adopted a new persona.

I stand by the stage, feeling I too have come alive again. The closing act gets ready. The blues band, Jubal, joins Brazilian drummers, a didgeridoo player, an Indian singer and a famous bouzouki player from Lesbos. Their triumphant finale will be the festival's parting statement.

It's the night before the elections and SS polls are down. The concert is being broadcast live on national television. The stage lights up for the cameras.

I'm approached by a woman with long, dark hair, dressed in a white robe. The old ad for the harmonica school has finally delivered.

"Sita?"

"Not any more. You'll find another muse if you continue the Journey."

"You were there at Ithaca Road, Copacabana, the Taj Mahal, Arthur's Seat?"

"Also, my husband ran the Apollo School of Music."

"The Seven Steps?"

"You might have even seen him in an old Marlon Brando movie."

"Does that mean that...?"

She stops me with a kiss on both cheeks.

"You'll work it out when you write all this."

She hands me a small bundle of white silk.

"You lost this a long time ago, Chris."

As I look down, she leaves and passes through the crowd beyond the threshold of the lawns. A silver-haired man waits on a large white motorbike. She climbs on the back. It roars to a start and takes off. Her robe flows in the wind. She waves and disappears.

I unswathe the bundle. A chromatic 64 smeared with dried blood. Balanced in my hand, I feel an old, familiar charge. I blow a note. It soars through the air like a condor. Heads turn towards me. I feel a tap on my shoulder and look up.

It's the bass player from a group about to perform. Gary's son, Jason.

"We're kicking off with Key to the Highway."

He points to the seven steps by the stage.

"I think it's time to join us."

Tamám shud

ACKNOWLEDGEMENTS

Many thanks to the Cosmos Co-op team of Marco V Morelli, Geoffreyjen Edwards, Mary Thaler, and Kayla Morelli for bringing this fantasy to life.

To Suzanne, my Camino companion on the road to Santiago de Compostela, and Max my biker buddy in Vietnam, your childhoods were the greatest journey of them all.

ABOUT THE AUTHOR

The son of a Polish cavalry officer, Richard Andrews grew up in Australia before moving to Canada. In between, he chalked up more than 40 years as a journalist, foreign correspondent, diplomat and freelancer. His work and travels have taken him from piranha fishing on the Amazon and hopping freight trains across the desert to Fortune 100 boardrooms and playing guitar in a Beijing nightclub. An award-winning editor, he now teaches at McGill University and lives on a former vineyard in Quebec's Eastern Townships.

Untimely Books is an independent publisher of literary works that illumine the mind, question the contemporary, and reimagine horizons of thought, feeling, and action for a planetary age. As an imprint of Cosmos Cooperative (a creative community and member-owned publishing platform) and *Metapsychosis* (a journal of consciousness, literature, and art), Untimely Books serves as a conduit for diverse forms of writing by Cosmos members, including original works of fiction, poetry, philosophy, essays, and memoir.

untimelybooks.com